CHRISTABEL

Karin Kallmaker

Bella
BOOKS
2008

Bella Books, Inc.
P.O. Box 10543
Tallahassee, FL. 32302

First Edition: Naiad Press 1998
First Bella Books Revised Edition 2008

This novel was originally released under the pen name Laura Adams in 1998 by The Naiad Press. This second edition has been augmented with substantial additional text and contains editorial changes from the original.

Printed in the United States of America on acid-free paper

Cover designer: Linda Callaghan

ISBN 10: 1-59493-134-8
ISBN 13: 978-1-59493-134-5

In memory of Jeannette H. Foster

whose analysis of Samuel Coleridge's *Christabel* made me realize there was a different story to tell; a young woman falling under the spell of a beautiful witch is not necessarily a bad thing.

Halley's Comet appeared in 1682. Edmond Halley identified it as a naturally recurring phenomenon. The rampantly superstitious Puritans were not so scientific.

.

About the Author

The author of more than twenty romances and fantasy-science fiction novels, Karin Kallmaker's repertoire includes the award-winning *Just Like That, Maybe Next Time, Sugar* and *18th & Castro*. Short stories have appeared in anthologies from publishers like Alyson, Bold Strokes, Circlet and Haworth, as well as novellas and short stories with Bella Books. She began her writing career with the venerable Naiad Press and continues with Bella.

Karin's work can be found at www.bellabooks.com. Details and background about her novels and upcoming works can be found at kallmaker.com.

Chapter 1

It had finally stopped raining.

Mud slopped into Christabel's boots, but her feet were already so cold and wet it made no difference. She could have saved herself from some of the muck if she had used the sidewalk, but boots scuffing on wood this late at night might make someone curious.

Her mind was churning with fear over what she was about to do. Force of habit was the only reason she remembered to cross the street before she passed the Dawson's house. The Dawson family refused to accept the new ways in the colony, in spite of Lord Berkeley's order to the contrary, and clung to the habits of the land of their birth—well, just about everybody's birth. In London, all types of refuse, from kitchen offal to chamber waste, were flung out the windows into the street. No one ever walked in front of the Dawson house. It was a disgrace, her father said. Mr. Albright, who had the Lord Berkeley's ear, hinted that come summer the Dawsons could find themselves deported.

All the houses she passed, big and small, were shuttered against the bitter night, but some lamplight peeked through. It wasn't enough to reveal her quiet but rapid passage through the rain-soaked streets. She was just a dark figure on a dark night, perhaps just a trick of the wind.

It didn't take long to wend her way past the millpond and through the sluice gate. It was the only way out of the township fort without going through the gates or by boat. She was soaked from the hips down when she scrambled up the side of the creek. In the distance she could hear the steady roar of the Hudson River, running fast and strong. It had been a wet but not freezing winter so far; there was no sign of any ice on the water's surface.

She reevaluated the temperature once she was out of the millpond. The wind was like a frozen knife through her wet clothes, and her first few steps revealed ice slivers forming on the puddles. Ma always said that January was worse than December—she was right, as usual.

When she came abreast of the entrance to the Governor's estate, Christabel stopped to get her bearings. The iron fence and heavy gates were fettered with chains and ropes, which, as she drew closer, turned into the barren stems of Lady Berkeley's English roses. It was hard to believe the fallow, dank fields would yield corn and tulips come spring. She was not pursued, nor was there any sign of a watch at the gates. The night was too bitter for anyone to believe that a girl her age would sleep out-of-doors. It was unthinkable. That was why she was going to do it.

She was going to prove that being born here in the colony made her tougher and stronger and smarter than any sissified brat from England. If Pa and men like him hadn't helped the Duke of York take all of New Amsterdam from the Dutch, her ladyship Bitsy Albright wouldn't even be here. Bitsy Albright might have a fancy lace collar and a pair of fine linen hose but she was not Queen Mary for all the airs she gave herself.

For all her self-satisfied ways, Bitsy was dying to find out if what that old native woman had told her cousin about the Witching Tree was true. That if a young girl slept under it for one night she would dream of her true love. The old woman hadn't called it the Witching Tree. That was Bitsy's name for it. But Bitsy was too cowardly to find out for herself.

She was going to sleep under the tree and show Bitsy and her gaggle of giggling friends for the cowards they were. She knew she wasn't going to dream any nonsense about true loves and weddings—she wasn't interested in any of the boys. They were callow clods, every single one of them. Billy Buckley was the only one she even remotely liked, because he had some guts. The idea of sharing a bed with him, doing any of the mystifying things that Bitsy giggled knowingly about, but wouldn't describe, well, that just wasn't going to happen with any boy in town. Billy Buckley wasn't going to be in her dreams. She wasn't going to dream. She never did.

She guessed she'd been plodding along for about an hour when she left the last outbuilding of Peter Stuyvesant's huge Bouwerie behind. Why the former Dutch governor of the colony hadn't gone home again was a mystery. He could have easily sold the estate. He was on good terms with Lord Berkeley, even though Lord Berkeley had been the leader of the invasion fleet that had taken New Amsterdam—now New York and New Jersey—from the Dutch colonizers.

Christabel wondered what it must feel like to have something you'd built with your own two hands taken away from you just because someone else had five hundred soldiers, a small fleet of ships and the patronage of the powerful Duke of York behind him. Of course, Peter Stuyvesant's militia had wrested the lower island from the Manhattan people to start with. She'd mentioned that to Pa once, and he'd said we'd all be gone and buried before anyone could say for a certainty who would rule this little bit of land. It wasn't as if it was a very important location.

Some of the other Dutch families had lingered as well, mostly the merchants who had good trade and good sense to deal with the new English settlers fairly. The Roosevelts still got the finest linens from Europe, and Pa said if you wanted a house built, the Rikers were the best you could do.

The wood thickened as Christabel made her way toward the center of the island. The bony fingers of bare sugar maples reached for her—but that was just nonsense, she told herself

3

sternly. Reverend Gorony could preach all he wanted about demons and devil spawn, but she didn't believe it. If all was His creation, surely God had better things to do than create evil creatures. She thought they were just stories to scare people. Well, she wasn't scared.

She stifled a scream when an owl hooted near her, and she struggled faster through the mud. Even in the dark she knew she could find the tree. When they picked berries in the summer it was a favorite place to gather and eat because it was unmistakable: a lone oak in a forest of pines and sugar maples. Its low branches invited climbing. She had climbed to the top once, but the whipping that had followed when Ma found out had made her give up climbing. It wasn't fair. Billy Buckley hadn't gone up nearly as high as she had, and everyone had made a big fuss over it. None of them had known that the natives thought the tree had magic in its roots.

Reverend Gorony would have her pilloried if he ever found out she had given a moment's thought to what was surely devil's mischief. If the native women believed the tree held magic, that was an unmistakable sign of Satan's influence—the Manhattans were godless and unclean. The women were indecently attired most of the time. Reverend Gorony said their presence made the island a breeding ground for Satan. Only the ones who had accepted the Church were welcome inside the gates. He'd said so just last Sunday. He'd been so adamant about it, most of the merchants had taken to buying their goods—furs, venison and fish, mostly—outside the township proper.

The native wickedness had never seemed certain to Christabel. She was the eldest of the colony-born English children, and she was no more wicked than the English-born ones. Perhaps that's why she wasn't particularly afraid of the natives. Bitsy and Cherry squealed and ran for cover if one of the men even walked in the street. And as far as wickedness goes, she'd noticed that, for all of Reverend Gorony's warnings about their temptations, plenty of the menfolk didn't bother to avert their eyes when a woman Manhattan rode astride.

She slopped on through the muck and rotting leaves. The track was rutted and full of puddles she couldn't see even when she was up to her ankles in them. When she lifted her sopping feet, her boots made a horrible sucking sound as if the frigid ground wanted to swallow her whole.

By the time she turned toward the spacious grove where the oak tree was centered, Christabel was shaking with cold. She was worried, too, about how to explain the condition of her clothes to her mother. She hadn't realized it would be so muddy. She was supposed to be sleeping at Bitsy's tonight. Goodwife Albright would never have let Christabel get so filthy and then sleep on her fine sheets. She would have to think of a way to explain it. Maybe she could say she fell. They lived only a few houses down from Bitsy, but she could say she went across the street to speak with someone. Wait, it would be even better to say she'd felt the need to pray when she woke, so she skipped breakfast and went around to Canal Street to the new church to kneel for a while. Then she fell on her way home.

That might work. Any sign of piety on her part would be heartily welcomed by her parents.

There. Finally, the track widened and she was in the oak's clearing. The tree stood a good thirty feet from any other, with a spreading canopy that cast cool, moist shade in summer. A sudden noise from the depths of the darkness under the tree brought another yelp to her throat, but it quickly died when a family of deer shuffled quietly out of sight, leaving the clearing to her.

She loved to picnic here in the summer. She always felt safe here—maybe that was why she hadn't hesitated to answer Bitsy's dare. Through the oak's barren branches she could see stars glittering coldly. Pa knew the names of some of the stars. Reverend Gorony said girls didn't need to know such things, so Pa had stopped teaching her about them. But she picked out the Little Dipper and was somehow comforted by that, until she looked just above it and saw the smear of red-white light that had appeared in the last few weeks, very faint. Reverend Gorony said it was an ill omen, a sure sign of God's disfavor for the wickedness of pagan Catholicism, of the idolatry of the Anglicans. She'd heard Pa telling Ma after church that the Reverend had exceptional eyes to know the comet was meant to scare Catholics and Anglicans, not Puritans. Still, it made her afraid to look at it. If the heavens could change, was there anything that couldn't?

Now that she was here, looking at stars and scaring herself served no useful purpose. What was she going to do? She had to be asleep to dream, but she was too chilled to sleep. It didn't help that the wind was rising a little. She pulled her cloak more tightly around her. It was cold, she thought, but not so cold she couldn't stand it. Her thick woolen gown might not be the latest in fashion but it was warm where it wasn't wet.

The wind died, and the wood fell into a hush. Even the leaves stilled. It was as if the trees were holding their breath.

I am not afraid, Christabel told herself. There were no bears on the island any more. The Dutch had known how to make it safe. The Manhattans were confined to a settlement on the northern tip of the island, too. The colony was small, but beautiful. Pa said there were some houses as big as a Duke's up on the Hudson River in New York proper. Lord Berkeley's main estate was up there. The Dutch had built snug homes and wide streets, even some canals to bring fresh water from the rivers. They had left behind sturdy buildings with good outhouses and neatly tended farms, and a town center with a good wharf that had supported the Dutch West Indies Company's trade. Merchants did well during warmer weather.

The Albrights even had a pump in the house, but then their well was right near. When Lord Berkeley gave Pa his land grant for service, Pa had picked a smaller place on the island because of all the good wells and clean river water. They had a nice house, bigger than most military families, and the land was Pa's, not just leased from the Lord. A commoner owning land—well, that was why lots of folks from home were heading to the colony.

She jumped up and down for a while, trying to get tired enough to go to sleep. It helped warm her up a little. The still of the surrounding wood continued and, not for the first time,

Christabel wondered if some of the Manhattans were night-hunting nearby. No, she would not think about that. She was all alone.

Abruptly, the wind whipped up again and the stars disappeared behind a low cloud. It might rain, but she didn't think so. She was feeling better. Warm, almost. It was time to sleep.

She curled up in a shallow root hollow sheltered from the wind by the trunk. She was getting very sleepy. And at last she was warm.

The warmth was coming from the tree. The tree shed light on her. The light was as green as new summer grass, and she relaxed into wakeful dreams.

Her mother scolded her for running, for scuffing her boots, for ripping her dress. Pa said she was more fearless than any England-born son of a lord. Until Reverend Gorony built the new church, he'd said it with a gleam of pride in his eye, but not lately.

Ma talked about getting married. That wasn't a dream; that was a memory. Bitsy talked of nothing else. Christabel dreamed of Bitsy in her best dress, the fanciest the Church would allow, getting married to Tom Sherman. She tried to dream of her own wedding, of her own true love. But even as her dreams turned to all the boys she knew and even to all the men who were just names—kings and dukes and lords—she pushed them out and dreamed of dancing under the tree while hot flames from a bonfire threw themselves against the sky. She dreamed of a warm summer night and laughter.

Fantastic creatures from Pa's Greek stories flitted across her mind and she woke briefly, smiling. Pa had been to Greece long ago and had shown her the place on the big map he kept wrapped in oilskin. Pa used to tell her travel stories and let her read his books about them, that is, until Reverend Gorony had said that women didn't need to read and if they did, the Good Book was plenty. Last year only boys had been going to the church school, and she'd had to give back her *New England Primer*.

She dreamed of having a dinner consisting only of books,

but no matter how many she ate she still felt hungry. A centaur prowled the wood nearby; a naiad swam in the river. Deep in the warm tree, a dryad breathed. Surely these wonderful beings dwelled on these shores, too. The natives believed every thing had a spirit, even clouds and smoke and deer, even the sun and the rain. She wondered what the natives called spirits of trees. She dreamed that the dryad in the tree awoke, and wrapped its arms around her to keep the cold away.

Her sleep deepened, and she drifted in memories and remembered her daydreams. The light around her softened to the color of old moss fringed with black lashes, and she dreamed that the tree blinked.

Chapter 2

Dina Rowland stuffed the last of her notes and the extra copies in her briefcase and hightailed it after the rest of the group. Even though she seethed at being left behind to clean up, her smile was bright and easy as she joined The Boys at the elevator.

"That went well, I think," Doug Trenton ventured.

Elliott Brinks, ever the kiss-ass, agreed. "We knocked their socks off."

"They left the room before we did," Dina observed after the elevator started its descent. "They didn't want to discuss anything among themselves."

"And that is not good," George Berkeley pronounced. His opinion was final. "As usual, Dee, you're right on. Your presentation was killer, even if the client is a moron."

"Doug did the graphs," Dina said to be fair, but she cracked a lopsided smile at George. She liked him immensely—he wasn't the one who had left her behind to clean up. Doug and Elliott were her peers and should have helped out. They were too stupid to know that George had noticed their arrogant assumption that the woman in the group cleaned up. George didn't miss anything; he read people as easily as he read the marquee in Times Square.

His intuition had made him rich. He was beginning to respect Dina's intuition as well. She had been dead right for a lot of deals in the last couple of years.

Fifth Avenue was treacherous with open umbrellas. She struggled to open her own, and then gratefully accepted shelter under George's. She saw the look Doug and Elliott exchanged. Like almost everyone else, they thought she and George were lovers. She readily told anyone who would listen that she was a lesbian, but having no partner to point to, or even a passing girlfriend or two, didn't help her case. Most people preferred to think sex, not talent, was the reason Dina stood so high in George's estimation.

Her feet were drenched within moments, and they'd only just dried out from the trip here. Dina and George waited for Doug, who had to have his fix at the ubiquitous coffee bar on the corner. Elliott managed to hail a cab, and they scrunched together for the nine-block journey to the offices of Berkeley & Holland Investments and Capital. Except for the rain, Dina would have walked and arrived there ahead of the cab, which, after a five-block detour, finally deposited them on Church Street outside their office.

George didn't seem inclined to rehash the meeting with the moronic never-to-be-clients. They wanted to take their company public and hadn't cared for Berkeley & Holland's conservative estimates of how rich they would get and the long list of *ifs* that had precluded getting rich. Without a doubt some other firm had promised them the sky, and with a great deal of luck, these people might actually have a positive initial public offering. But Berkeley & Holland didn't believe in luck, and they weren't so hungry that they wanted to risk their industry-leading record with IPOs. Millionaire-making IPOs had tailed off in the mid-1990s and had yet to recover.

Dina kicked off her wet shoes in the office and spread her damp coat over the couch. Her assistant, Jeff Blake, took the briefcase from her hand. "I'll take care of these. You've got sixteen messages, and the designer will be here in five minutes."

"We took a cab," Dina said, which explained their lateness. Even in her stockings she was three inches taller than Jeff, but he never seemed to mind looking up. Eliot always seemed afraid to look her in the eye because of the five inches she had on him.

"Rotten presentation?"

"Not rotten, pointless. What's that designer's name again?"

"Leonard Goranson." Jeff's exasperated tone implied that Dina should have remembered. He pointed to his shirt front. "Imported. See? A college buddy who works for Coca-Cola in London acquired it for me."

Dina scrutinized the tiny lettering. "Oh. So he designed that shirt?"

"The man is a genius. It's the only thing I have of his, and it took six months to pay for it."

"Are you sure you're straight?"

Jeff rolled his eyes. "Not every well-dressed man in this town is gay. We don't have time for chitchat, either."

"Tyrant." She sipped the plain, hot coffee she found on her desk. "You're a damned good tyrant, though. You treat me well."

"And vice versa." Having emptied her briefcase of presentation detritus headed for the shredder, Jeff whisked back to his workstation outside her door. He was a maniac with both eyes on Dina's office as his future home. However, Jeff seemed to understand the only way to get Dina's office was to find Dina another one—one on the partners' floor, for instance. Other assistants would have been busy stabbing her in the back, but it wasn't Jeff's style. Dina had mentioned Jeff often to George. George liked loyalty in people. If she did move up to partner, God please let it be soon, Jeff also had a very good shot at moving up.

She returned two phone calls and finished the coffee before Jeff buzzed.

"Goranson is running late. He wants to meet you at the storefront. This means I risked wearing this shirt for nothing."

Dina's sigh was as tired as Jeff's. The rain had not let up. "Get me directions."

Jeff leaned in a few minutes later. "Goranson's assistant is a rude little shit, just so you know. The *gallery* is going to be located two blocks down from Bergdorf Goodman. Fifty-fifth Street at Fifth Avenue. You do know where Bergdorf's is, don't you, ducks?"

Dina laughed at Jeff's brutal rendition of a Manchester accent. "I do. Pricey district. No wonder Goranson needs capital. And it's a gallery, not a store?"

"Goranson sells art, apparently, not clothing."

"I'll remember that."

And she would, too. LG Incorporated was her bambino to make into a gold mine. It was her ticket to the partners' floor. If she made partner, she might actually be able to take a weekend off. She could even get something that amounted to a life. She was getting past the young-and-hungry stage. Dina repacked her briefcase with the Goranson file and the work she was taking home. Her PDA and voice recorder fit neatly into the pockets designed for them.

"Want me to meet you downstairs with a sandwich? You can eat it in the cab."

"I'm walking over to the subway," Dina said. "A cab will take forever. Don't worry, mother, I'll eat something after the meeting with Goranson."

"If you die while I'm your assistant, no one is going to promote me." Jeff excelled at pragmatism.

"I ate lunch," Dina began in her defense, then faltered. "Oh. That was yesterday, wasn't it? Well, I'll eat a big dinner."

Jeff was clearly unconvinced, but went back to work on the Doering prospectus.

Once on the street, Dina ruthlessly raised her umbrella and shoved her way into the subway-bound foot traffic. As she eased into the tide of rushing people, she concentrated on avoiding umbrella spikes. The steps to the subway were slick and treacherous, but she was able to squeeze her way onto the second uptown-bound train. She spent the entire journey with someone's elbow jammed into her ribs and a briefcase scraping the back of one knee. As always in the subway, she followed the social rules: no eye contact. You never knew when someone was waiting for that to signal their personal apocalypse.

At Fifty-seventh Street she struggled back up to the surface against the tide of tourists and commuters. Fifth Avenue's wide sidewalks were packed building to curb with scowling commuters scurrying home after a long week of sodden work. Dina's stomach rumbled—she wanted her cozy chair and a bowl of hot soup.

The street smelled like wet wolfhound and diluted urine. Manhattan only looked poetic from the second floor or higher. The smell of the street would cling to her, which was depressing since she had taken special care with her wardrobe this morning so as not to appear unlearned to this designer person. Her Donna Karan suit was now rumpled and wet, but it was still a timeless Donna Karan original. Her shoes were soaked, and they pinched her feet, but the Italian leather still looked good.

She passed Bergdorf's with a brief but longing gaze at a thick cashmere sweater in the window. She had thought that every inch of this district—one of the most famous and lucrative shopping areas in the world—was occupied with waiting lines for leases. You couldn't ask for a better location, and with retail the three top priorities were location, location, location.

She turned the corner at Fifty-fifth and surveyed the street. It was not quite as posh as Fifth Avenue proper. Gucci, Trump Tower and Tiffany's were all hard to compete with. But the corner building was eye-catching, which might account for why she had never noticed the building next to it. It wasn't that it was nondescript, but she just found no reason to look at it. She focused on the display windows and realized she couldn't see through the glass.

She blinked and felt dizzy for a second, then shook her head. Not now, she thought. She didn't care that her mother had warned her, she still didn't believe she'd inherited some sort of so-called "gift." Since her mother's death three years ago, she'd been having...*flashes*, for want of a better word. Flashes of intuition and prescience.

In the last hours of her life, her mother had told Dina that the gift passed from eldest daughter to eldest daughter, usually after death. Dina had not believed it. Still didn't. She took a deep breath and ignored the heaviness that washed over her as she approached the building. The place made her skin crawl, and she wasn't even inside.

At closer range, of course, she could see into the display windows. But beyond was impenetrable. The place was downright scary, a bad image for a store. Remember, she told herself, this isn't a store. It's a *gallery*. No doubt many cosmetic changes were planned for the exterior, and once done she was sure the building would be fine. It would be *fine*.

She shook off the nonsensical prickles of fear and pushed her way through the door, which was propped open with a box. She gratefully dumped her saturated umbrella on the floor next to several others. There were no lights, but she heard voices, as if people were just out of sight in the darkness. No wonder the windows had seemed dark—they were. Nothing sinister about it.

Her voice echoed. "Hello? Mr. Goranson? It's Dina Rowland from Berkeley and Holland."

Light abruptly flooded the foyer, and there was a cheer from the group of men at the rear of the first floor. Dina was temporarily dazzled. When her vision cleared, she looked around her with appreciation. Whoever had had the space before had done a nice job—she stood in a three-story atrium. A spiral staircase with gleaming brass banisters coiled upward. She took a deep breath and shook off the last of the heebie-jeebies she'd picked up from the exterior.

She quickly focused on the three men walking toward her. Man one: black, close-cropped hair, off-the-rack suit, metal briefcase. The construction engineer, probably. Man two: not just white but translucent, swishy, designer suit, shirt looking similar to Jeff's but probably costing twice as much, sheaf of papers. The obnoxious assistant probably. Because man three, with the shoulder-length hair caught back in a ponytail, bronzed skin, and soft black leather pants and matching jacket, screamed *artiste* with every step. Dina was taken aback. Leonard Goranson was damned attractive, and he knew it.

His handshake was cold and two seconds too long. He was perhaps an inch taller, but he was trying to make it seem more. The assistant didn't bother. Jason Williams was indeed the construction engineer. His handshake was warm and hearty as he reminded Dina of his previous work with other B and H clients.

During her brief chat with Williams, Dina sensed Goranson's gaze on her, evaluating her clothes and her body. She was sure he did it to everyone, but she found his lack of subtlety annoying.

"So we were just in the process of finding the lights," Williams was saying. "I haven't seen the entire structure yet."

"Why don't we have a tour?" Goranson's voice was as cultured and accented as any Shakespearean actor's, but it was slightly flavored with an ever-present smugness. She already didn't like this guy, but she told herself to get over it. She reminded herself that becoming a partner at B and H was very, very important to her, making Goranson important to her. Her personal feelings didn't enter into it.

The narrow building was ideal for a haute couture establishment. With only three floors above ground level, it was too small for a lot of inventory, especially when the retail space had to be uncluttered. There would be no crowded rounds of clothing or tables with bargains in Goranson's gallery.

She took some notes while Goranson expounded on his decorating theme and more when Williams made comments about structural changes that might be needed.

They returned to the ground floor and headed for the basement. After some fumbling, Williams found the lights and they made their way into the most depressing gray room Dina had ever seen.

"We'll make some changes here, too. Even if it's just the accounting people, a client may wander down here." Goranson made it plain that only what clients thought mattered.

"Where does this go?" Dina gestured at another door that

looked as if it might be at the top of another flight.

Williams consulted some blueprints. "That's a sub-basement. Might be useful for secure records storage. Let's take a look."

Dina swallowed when she heard the drip of water after Williams opened the door. She let the three men go ahead, which turned out to be a good idea since she was overcome with dizziness as she crossed the threshold. She gripped the banister and prayed no one noticed before she could get herself under control.

She took four or five deep breaths, and then opened her eyes slowly. The light was dim and the room small. The walls, in addition to the floor, were unfinished concrete. The source of the water-drip and damp smell was a section of concrete that had cracked, letting a few roots curl in. Roots to what—just thinking about it made her dizzy again. The room itself wasn't a problem. It held echoes of dull business. But beyond the walls something... something was... Dina shook her head violently and retreated through the door behind her.

The dizziness immediately faded. She should have eaten something, that was all.

"Are you all right?" Goranson's solicitous tone snapped Dina back to reality.

"I'm fine. I get a little claustrophobic."

"No reason for you to go down there again, then."

She guessed that most women melted at the merest sign of his concern, but she knew his concern was for the millions Dina could bring by way of investors, not for any discomfort she might feel. A warning bell sounded in her mind—it was not her mother's "gift" helping her, just simple intuition. It would be a mistake to owe this man anything, even something as simple as a supportive hand at the back. She drew herself up to her full height and found a steady smile.

"It's going to take me about two weeks to do a complete report on the building," Williams was saying.

"I'll be back in London by then. Just fax it."

"Send me a copy, too," Dina said. She handed Williams her

card. "You know how we work."

"I'd prefer reviewing the information before it's sent to anyone else," Goranson said quickly.

Dina saw Williams hesitate, then look at her with a silent plea.

"Mr. Goranson," she began.

"Leonard, please."

She had to swallow hard to use his first name. It stung on the way through her mouth. "Leonard. Berkeley and Holland has a particular way of working. It's why we're who we are. We're not one of those firms that pastes their name on their client's work and sends it out to investors."

"I should hope not, given your fees." Charmingly said, but Goranson's gaze was flat.

"When I send out your prospectus to the investors, I will tell them in all honesty that I drew my conclusions and made my financial estimates based on direct—emphasis, direct—knowledge and receipt of information from people like Mr. Williams. The investor will have only my word that you had no undue influence over Mr. Williams's estimates of what it will take to ready this building for your gallery. I never lie to investors. It's bad business, and it's expensive to you in the end. Any hint of any sleight of hand on my part, and investors start raising their interest rates. That is, if they stay in the deal. And the stock investors will want to pay less."

"I understand. May I call you Dina?" At her nod, he continued. "Then we'll receive information simultaneously? You'll want to be present at initial meetings with furnishers, decorators, the stateside representatives from my textile suppliers?"

"Yes to all," Dina said. "It's how B and H does business. I'll also have to personally see your assets that you're pledging as security—I know you're not securitizing the entire investment, but what assets you are going to pledge I'll need to examine myself."

For some reason, this statement made Goranson smile. Dina repressed a shudder. "I think I can arrange that."

"Great," Dina said with what she hoped came across as enthusiasm. "Just get me a list of the assets and I'll arrange to verify them."

"Make a note, Gerrard." Goranson gestured at his assistant, who did make a note, all the while giving Dina a look that said the effort he was going to was all her fault.

"Thank you. I intend to make this transaction my number one priority, Leonard. George Berkeley will personally review everything I produce, as well."

Very good, then." Goranson glanced at the heavy gold watch on his wrist. "I've got an engagement to run to. It just came up this afternoon."

"Leo?"

Everyone turned to the soft voice behind them. For the third time in the last hour, Dina was stricken with vertigo. Surely it was just hunger and fatigue. PMS, maybe. Through the shoulders of the men she saw a woman, or a girl, no, a woman. Her dark eyes were huge and her skin alabaster with rose-stained cheeks and lips. She seemed like a mist, almost as if she wasn't there. But as she moved down the stairs with a flowing grace that mesmerized Dina, she solidified in Dina's mind. She had to be a model, but unlike most models, there was nothing boyish or waiflike about her. She was all woman, lushly female.

"You wanted to examine my assets?" Goranson gestured at the newcomer, who stood at the bottom of stairs. "This is my chief asset, la Christabel."

Dina looked at Goranson and knew that he understood assets were something you owned. That was when she began to hate him.

Leo looked at me speculatively, trying to figure out how to best make use of me. Not for gain, but for idle amusement during what he called a deadly dull trip. He glanced at the woman next to him. Ah, I was to be used for her distress.

I looked at her for the first time.

It was as if a million candles flashed in my eyes. It took all my strength not to flinch. I never let Leo see me flinch anymore. But my eyes could hardly bear to look at her, she was so bright.

I am used to fog. In a world of gray only dark and light are visible. I am draped in dark shadows. But then I saw *her*. Saw her with more than my eyes, with senses I hadn't known I possessed.

By her light I could see so many things clearly for the first time: Gerrard's sharp little teeth, his twitching nose. And Leo— in her light I could barely stand to look at him. So charming on the surface, but his flesh was pulled tight over a hungry and insatiable darkness.

She was looking at me now. I saw why Leo was so pleased with himself. He saw her light, and I was going to be used to bend the light to his way. If her light wouldn't bend, he would extinguish it. Darkness was his specialty.

She was walking toward me, Leo having said something about not being able to show me around the town tonight and putting her in the awkward position of agreeing to show me the sights. We'd been here several days; I hardly needed an escort. Our schedule was also very tight and none of the models had much in the way of social time. Apparently, I was expected to make time for Ms. Rowland.

I didn't protest. It was pointless—Leo would have his way. And I found myself wanting her light closer to me.

I don't believe in holy things anymore. I don't think I ever did, but if I'd clung to any belief in divine aid, Leo had driven it out of me.

Leo had proven to me how powerless holy things are. And she was not a holy being; it was not a saint who asked me if I liked museums. But her light came from some source that Leo could never tap, a place I would never go. I could only nourish the hope that she wasn't harmed by my selfish desire to warm myself near her.

I turned from the dark cold of the building, from Leo's disdain and Gerrard's disgust, and followed her into the watery light of early evening.

19

Chapter 3

"I like art," I assured Dina. As we got farther from the building, Dina's light faded until she was just a woman trying to stay dry under an umbrella not quite broad enough to protect both of us. Her head tipped toward me as she listened, but her gaze was fixed on the street. "Especially modern art. I was hoping to go to the Museum of Modern Art while I am here."

"I love MOMA." Her voice was like bells on the wind. "Have you eaten?"

"I'm a model," I said, laughing. "What do you think?"

She grinned as she tried yet again to hail a cab. "I think that's sad."

"So do I. And I'm hungry." Abruptly, it was true. Being near her had already nourished me enough to care about the persistent gnaw in my stomach. It wasn't just her, I told myself. Spending time with any woman was like water in the desert. Leo knows that I crave the company of women, and so he surrounds me with men or other models, whose competitive bitchiness leaves me just as drained.

"The food at the museum restaurant is expensive enough to keep us thin," she said, then blushed.

"Dina." I felt a strange thrill when I said her name. "I don't count enjoyment by how much it costs." I wanted to say I was not a bimbo. I wanted to say that most models are shrewd businesswomen, just as she appeared to be. I had certainly made my share of bargains. Best not mention that—some had turned out very bad in the end.

She looked relieved. "I'm sorry, that was a rude assumption on my part. And I didn't mean to sound like a cheapskate. I'm still a starving student at heart, I guess. I was taught the value of money by my mother." Her voice dropped slightly with tenderness. Plainly, she loved her mother. "Money is only good for the good you can do with it."

"Do you fight about how to use money? There—a cab." We simultaneously signaled, and the taxi screeched to a halt. A man tried to get there before us, but Dina made it to the door a split second before him, then I did...*it*. The slow blink into his bemused gaze, one shoulder back, and one hip rolling toward him so he inevitably glanced down at my legs—like nine men out of ten, his jaw went slack.

"Pardon me," he said, and he held the door, closing it after watching me hungrily into my seat.

Dina was trying to look lighthearted, but failed as she asked, "Does that happen to you all the time?"

"Usually when I want it to. Does that shock your sensibilities?"

She was serious now, and not looking at me. Damn Leo. I was already under her skin and already hating myself for the distress I would surely bring her. There was no other possible outcome. "That depends. I guess my mother would have said that looks like yours are only good for the good they can do."

"Your mother was a wise woman, but she didn't live in my world." Dina's light was too strong to have been exposed to anything in my world.

"If you mean she wasn't beautiful, you're wrong. My mother was an incredibly beautiful woman."

Like her daughter, I wanted to say. Green eyes like a summer lake were framed by dark lashes. Braided black hair that was no miracle of a salon, features that would age with character and strength, a long throat that would always be elegant but never haughty—she held herself with natural grace. No model could copy it. Like me, and it was ironic to think we had something in common, much of what she was had come to her from her mother. Unlike me, her beauty would strengthen into old age, instead of fading into limpness like an overblown hothouse flower.

"Actually, I meant the place I grew up. A little bit of nowhere in the middle of miles and miles of one-story nothing—Los Angeles. Ever been there?"

Dina shook her head. "My mother grew up on the Lower East Side. Not miles and miles of nothing, but block after block of it, sometimes forty stories high. But she stayed and cared and tried to bring in some fresh air. I grew up in that part of the city. I didn't move until I went to college."

Nothing I'd seen in New York compared to the desolation and hopelessness of the Los Angeles wasteland. "Did she use her looks for good?"

Dina's voice grew tight. "She didn't...use them."

"Of course she did. Everyone uses their birthright. Looks, brains, brawn, name." I managed to catch her gaze and hold it before she retreated behind her lashes.

"Do you use yours for good?"

"No," I said, flatly. "Leo uses them. I'm just the brain they're attached to."

Her opinion of me as a jaded jet-setter was solidifying. Until I met Leo I had never left the arid and dead-end streets of the ineptly named City of Industry where movie studios and costume houses dotted the landscape with their dilapidated facades. There was nothing glamorous about the movies except what an audience paid to see. I'd wasted several years trying to break into the biz, but the closer I got the more sordid it seemed. Leo had appeared the better choice.

I had been so wrong. But given the history of the women in my family, there were no right choices. Leo had taken me to London, Singapore, Brazil, and I'd seen them through a fog of darkness. I was the reason he had decided to design clothing for women, in addition to men. My body inspired him, he said, inspired his creativity. It inspired his cruelty, too.

I didn't want the first person who made my inner darkness lift just a little to think I was a spoiled and pampered brat, that my soul was as shallow as my blusher compact. Damn Leo, damn him. He had already made her wary of me.

The museum's coffee shop wasn't crowded. We went down the line to acquire sandwiches and coffee. Dina set the tray on a small table in the corner while I hung her umbrella from a spare chair to help it dry.

After slipping my coat onto the back of my chair I took my seat and realized she had frozen in the act of moving the sandwiches from the tray to the table.

"Sorry," she said quickly. She finished the task and sat down, her cheeks slightly tinged with pink.

"What?"

She shook her head as if it was nothing and I realized she was forcing herself not to look at me. I'd forgotten—Leo had said we were going to a cocktail party. The little black dress he'd designed for such occasions combined a high collar that looked demure with a keyhole bodice that was anything but. I hadn't realized how out of place I would look.

"I'll put my coat on."

"Don't—you don't have to. Silly of me." Dina's flush deepened. "I've never been this close to a model before, and I've always wondered how much was real." Her gaze flicked over me as if she couldn't help herself.

"All real," I said. "As real as anything can be with around-the-clock application of skin products, muscle toners, hair tints, body make-up—you name it. I'm covered with layers of fake."

"I don't believe you." She started to say the words lightly but it didn't end up that way.

A flirtatious answer—an invitation to find out, perhaps—died on my lips. Maybe I couldn't help my yearning to be near her, but given that I knew Leo had reasons for wanting us to spend time together, my actively seeking it out made me his accomplice. I would not be that to her. She had that look, almost bruised, that said I was disturbing her composure well beyond her comfort level.

She wasn't blaming me for it, yet. I did not want to give her cause to blame me, either.

We ate and talked of nothing important, deliberately on her part I think, and then took the elevator to the museum's third floor. I realized that while the brightness that came from Dina had faded, it still allowed me to see more clearly than I had since I was very young. It was as if I'd come out of a train tunnel, or had dark contacts rinsed from my eyes.

"This is my favorite room," Dina was saying, as she led me into a small chamber on the third floor. "I always like to start here."

I was shocked into surprised silence, not just by the beauty of the art, but by the way her taste mirrored my own. She had finally stopped looking at me from the corners of her eyes, and instead was raptly studying a vibrant Chagall she had probably seen a hundred times before. I liked that something so familiar could capture her attention so completely.

The only Chagalls I'd ever seen were in art books at the library. And here was *The Circus Rider*—the blue hurt my eyes. I could feel the yellow in my blood, while the red danced in my stomach. And the green was like...sanctuary.

The last words my mother had said to me before she died were, "Maybe you'll be the one to find green." That night, while I was asleep, she had hung herself. I was seventeen at the time, and her words had haunted me for the last eight years.

I studied the Chagall and drank in the vibrant, living green. The green was the color of Dina's eyes.

It was impossible not to watch Christa. Dina knew Christa was used to being stared at, used to be objectified and flattered, and the last thing Dina wanted was to join a queue of admirers.

"Around here." She led the way to the next gallery and paused just inside the door. "Another favorite."

"Oh my word." Christa took tiny steps forward, her lips parted in an almost childlike wonder as she gazed at *The Starry Night*. "You see pictures in books and it's nothing like this."

With Christa focused on the Van Gogh, Dina studied the open expression and the shimmer of amber light playing across Christa's brown eyes. A photograph in a magazine had little to do with reality in Christa's case as well. This was no empty-headed, body-obsessed socialite. Why was she tied up with a man like Goranson? Surely a dozen designers would vie for her talents. "You studied art in school?" Christa's expression stiffened slightly and she pushed her hands into the pockets of her coat. "No, at the library." She added, reluctantly, "I never finished high school. I was supporting myself from a pretty early age, and barely had enough money for rent, let alone television, books or movies. So I spent a lot of time at the library. I would study art or design or architecture—anything I liked."

"I'm glad to show you the real thing, then." Hadn't finished high school? Dina was willing to believe that Goranson made Christa feel ignorant and dependent. He'd tried to make her feel that way and Dina had no feelings of inferiority he could tweak. With a gesture at the painting, she said, "I love the color bursts against the deep blue."

"He was crazy—wonderfully crazy." Christa took another step closer. "Who knows what demons drove the poor man, but he produced such beauty."

She might have been describing Goranson and not Van Gogh, Dina realized. "He had a very troubled life and never rose above obscurity."

"Immortality often comes after death." Christa glanced over her shoulder at Dina, her face going into shadows. "Ironic, isn't it?"

"To say the least."

"But it's still immortality. Here we stand, admiring his work, and we know his name. In spite of the suffering in his life, we know his name." Christa went back to studying the painting, taking advantage of the shifting crowd around it to move forward until only a man and woman were between her and the canvas.

The man must have caught a glimpse of her out of the corner of his eye. He wasn't the first male Dina had watched go glassy-eyed and slack-jawed. She sincerely hoped she didn't have that expression on her face as well. She wanted to tell him he was lucky Christa had put her coat back on. He shifted out of Christa's way, pulling the woman at his side with him. "I'm not done," the woman said, and when he still nudged her, she gave him a dirty look to which he was utterly oblivious. Following his line of sight, the woman finally saw Christa, who seemed not to notice any of the interplay going on around her. Dina wasn't surprised when the woman gave her companion another dirty look. But she was startled when that look transferred to Christa with a spiteful edge.

"Fine," the woman snapped, turning on her heel. They were not out of earshot when Dina clearly heard her say, "Bitch."

She couldn't tell from Christa's expression if she had heard it. Christa'd done nothing, said nothing—hadn't even looked at either of the other people. Obviously, the other woman held Christa to blame for her boyfriend's tongue hanging out. For heaven's sake, what would the woman have done if Christa had actually smiled or flirted?

"It happens more often than you think," Christa said quietly. "What am I supposed to do, wear a garbage sack and dye my hair greasy gray? Put on fifty pounds and break my nose in a couple of places?"

"Of course not. I don't understand that kind of reaction."

"I do. If you believe beauty is a limited commodity, then you resent someone who seems to have more than their fair share. Jealousy and insecurity can turn anyone into a viper." Christa sighed. "Truth—all women are beautiful."

"Amen, sister," Dina said lustfully.

Christa smiled at that, as Dina had hoped she would. "I can't be a waitress. All it took was one guy who didn't like how I said no. Something always happened. I tried to work in offices, but they're filled with women like that one. It's my fault when married men hit on me, and so forth." The smile deepened. "Or married women. I tried to work in day care, hospices—places that are always hiring. It never worked out. Modeling is the only job I've ever had where the way I looked was an asset."

"The burden of a beautiful woman."

Christa drew back. "That's not funny."

"I'm sorry," Dina said quickly. "I'm not belittling your experience."

"It's not what most people would describe as tragic." Christa turned from the painting, her head down and hands still in her pockets. "Nobody's life is what it appears from the outside."

Dina was silent for a moment, then said softly, "I really didn't mean that the way it sounded."

Christa lifted her head then, and their gazes locked. "No, I don't believe you did."

Later, trying to sleep, Dina analyzed over and over that long, shared look. Her heart had been beating so loudly her vision pulsed. Christa's eyes seemed to say *Go away* and *Stay* at the same time. Then, in response to whatever had shown in Dina's expression, Christa had given her a desperate, pleading look. Was it simply *Not you too* or the far more likely *You don't have a chance, so don't even start?*

Her own reactions had made no sense, and even now, sleepless and strangely anxious, Dina couldn't sort out her feelings. Attraction, definitely, and she wasn't used to being so drawn to a woman, just like that. Maybe that was all it was, attraction to a supermodel and finding out she was no better than any red-blooded male. It was humbling to think she couldn't control her libido.

She finally took her mother's dreamcatcher off the peg next to her bed. It never failed to comfort her and, sure enough, within a few minutes she was yawning. An encounter with a celestial being, she murmured to herself, a creature of elusive beauty, was bound to be disturbing.

All in all, it was a good thing she was unlikely to see Christa again.

Chapter 4

The Great Mother was calling.

Her own mother had often, and with great weariness, pointed out that Rahdonee could hear the Great Mother beckoning from the farthest points of the island, but not hear a simple request that she clean up her latest concoction.

She missed her mother for all the reasons she had fought with her. After she passed her three nights with the spirit guide, she understood her mother's overprotectiveness and nagging for what they were—love and concern.

If her mother were still alive, she would be concerned that Rahdonee was undertaking a journey of several miles in the middle of a freezing winter night. Rahdonee would tell her not to worry, and they would fight. It would be so nice to walk that path one more time.

But since her mother's passing to the new circle, Rahdonee's path had been new and always changing. Tonight, she woke from deep sleep to hear the Great Mother calling her to the Sacred Tree. She gathered her bodeb, wrapped herself warmly, and set off at a sustainable trot.

Her tightly wrapped feet flew over the ground with the

lightness of a deer. She kept to the sides of the trail where the mud would not be as deep and turned unerringly at each fork to the path that led to the Sacred Tree.

If nothing came of her journey, she could always gather the leech plants that grew near the tree. Their medicine was useful for blistered skin and burns. But there was something there. The Great Mother wouldn't get her up in the middle of a night like this for nothing.

When she reached the clearing of the Sacred Tree, she was sweating hard but not really tired. Such journeys were routine for her and most of her people. Certainly a horse would have been faster, but she had none.

There was someone there in the clearing with her. The tranquility of the tree was disturbed. She drew closer, suspicious of white man's mischief—a trap or hunting net could be lurking.

She didn't see the bundle of clothing at the foot of the tree until she was almost upon it. She hurriedly unwrapped it, not willing to believe it was a person, so forlorn.

In horror she uncovered a girl, still and blue, and knew this was what she had been called to find.

Someone was shaking her, but if she woke up she would be cold again. Christabel closed her eyes tightly and willed away the insistent hand and voice.

Her hands were unwrapped from the edge of her cloak. Christabel was shocked awake by sudden heat in her fingertips. She gasped and found herself staring into outraged green eyes. After a moment's confusion, she realized her hands were trapped between the native woman's thighs.

She tried to snatch them away, but her body didn't listen. She couldn't feel anything except her hands and the icy chill of her breath through her nose.

The woman made a noise of satisfaction, bending to peer intently into Christabel's eyes. Christabel tried not to be afraid. She had no strength to protest as the woman unwrapped her cloak and removed her wet clothes. She could feel her wrists now, through a stinging prickle of pins. When her hands slipped away from the other woman's body, she wanted to cry out at the pain of the rapid return of cold. She managed to turn her head slightly—and did moan. Her fingers and arms were marbled with blue.

Was this woman stealing her clothes? She had never been naked in front of a stranger. She was going to die here—she'd been a fool. Her eyes were too cold to tear. She couldn't manage more than an incoherent whisper through her frozen lips.

The shock that followed was vividly painful. All at once the woman lifted her out of the hollow and drew Christabel's naked body against her own, wrapping them both in the voluminous fur that served as her cloak. The heat of the other woman's body pricked like needles against Christabel.

After a few minutes she found she could cry. The pins stabbing in her body intensified, and the stranger held her as she sobbed.

It was a long while before she realized the woman was speaking in English. "You will be warm, soon."

I'll never be warm again, Christabel thought. It seemed like forever since she had slipped out of Bitsy's house, but there was still no sign of dawn in the sky above them.

"Can you speak?"

Christabel cleared her throat experimentally, then croaked, "Yes, I'm better."

"Why are you here?"

There was a slight trilling, almost a ringing sound, when the native woman spoke.

"I am dreaming of my true love," she said, before she thought better of it. Surely the woman would think her crazy. Well, all things considered, she probably thought that already.

Instead, the woman laughed. "You've been told only half of the magic. You must sleep here on the long day. In summer."

"Oh," Christabel murmured. She was getting warm again, truly warm. "That makes more sense."

"Are you so desperate to know your true love's face?"

"No, I just wanted to show Bitsy and her friends that they're cowards."

"You are not a coward," the woman said, very softly. "But you are foolish. By morning you would have been dead. Thank the Great Mother I am here."

"Great Mother?"

The woman made a sound that could have been consternation. "I am sorry. Yours is not the way of the Great Mother. You are a child of the Christ."

"Well, I'm a Puritan."

"A Puritan clergyman taught me English," the woman explained. Christabel thought it was more to keep her awake than out of any necessity. "I studied his religion. I am Puritan also."

"You mean you accepted Christ as your savior?"

"What is Christ but the child of the Great Mother? All comes from her. It matters not to her that I say to the clergyman that I accept Christ as my savior. I hear the voice of the Great Mother. I want to understand white man's ways."

"Do you understand them?" Christabel wanted to say that she did not, but she didn't want to appear ignorant.

"No. I am often mystified. The Christ speaks of forgiveness and salvation through faith, but then I heard what happened to Eliza Albright."

Christabel nodded drowsily. She wasn't supposed to know about Bitsy's cousin, Eliza, but what she hadn't overheard from her parents she'd been supplied with by Bitsy. Eliza wasn't married, and her father had found out she was having a baby. She'd disgraced the entire Albright family. Bitsy's mother didn't make or receive calls for three whole weeks after the news had spread.

Christabel hadn't even realized that such a thing was possible. Eliza wouldn't tell who the man was, either. Reverend Gorony and some of the Elders had taken the baby away; Bitsy didn't know where. Eliza had spent three days in the stocks after the baby was born, and then been taken by boat in the middle of the night and left on the mainland, her face marked with charcoal to say that no man protected her. Eliza had never come back.

"What would the Great Mother have done to Eliza?"

"Loved her. Loved her baby. There is no sin in love."

"Reverend Gorony makes it sounds like all love is a sin, even if I love my parents. It's more important that I obey them than love them."

"I—I miss Reverend Downing. He was a wise man, much as the resting chief of my clan. I wished once to bring them together and help make talk. They would have liked each other."

"I miss him, too. He let me read." She felt so drowsy, and yet she knew she had to go home. "I think I can walk now. I have to get back before sunup."

The woman seemed to understand that necessity. She unfolded her cloak, and Christabel was oddly pleased to find that the woman was taller than she was—it got very tiring being the tallest girl in the entire town. The woman helped Christabel put on her freezing clothes and kept her moving when she wanted to just stand still and shiver.

"You have a long walk. I will go with you. You should eat this as we go." She offered a stick of dried meat wrapped with something that tasted vaguely lemony.

Remembering not to talk with her mouth full, Christabel said, "This is good. You don't have to walk with me," even though she longed for the company.

"I know. Stay to the edges of the path," the woman instructed, and they set off.

Christabel quickly realized that had she done that earlier she wouldn't be half as muddy. She'd stayed in the middle of the path because she had been afraid to be too close to the darkness of the trees. But with her guide following closely behind, she didn't mind at all.

"What's your name?"

"It was written down as Geraldine in the church Bible."

"That doesn't suit you," Christabel said. "What's your real name?"

"Rahdonee."

"That's pretty. Nicer than Bitsy."

"What is your name?"

"Christabel. My ma calls me Chrissy."

"That is also nicer than Bitsy."

Christabel laughed and was suddenly glad she had met Rahdonee. So she didn't dream of her true love. So what? She'd met someone smart and funny, qualities that Bitsy and the rest didn't possess in any great quantity.

"Mother deer," Rahdonee said, and sure enough a doe, heavy with fawn, ambled across the trail in front of them. It didn't seem to mind their presence at all. "That is a good omen," Rahdonee added.

Christabel remembered her question about the spirits of trees and found herself telling Rahdonee all about Greek creatures and absorbing every word Rahdonee said in return. The spirits of trees were called after the tree, as were the spirits of clouds and rivers. It was so much easier to remember, Christabel thought.

It was a surprise when the first buildings of the Bouwerie came into view. It seemed like they'd been walking only minutes.

"I can find my way from here," Christabel said. "I just follow the road now, and I know how to get back in without being seen."

"Are you certain?" Rahdonee didn't seem too eager to get much closer to the town.

"I can do it," Christabel insisted. The moon had risen fully, and the road was well lit compared to earlier. She glanced at Rahdonee and realized she hadn't really seen her face in the dark. Rahdonee couldn't be that much older than she was—but she seemed so wise.

"I've never seen an Indian with green eyes," she said.

"I am the daughter of the nordwek, who came to our island many, many lifetimes ago. None of them stayed, but their children are still with us. I am the only green one now, but more will follow me."

Christabel could see Rahdonee smiling in the dark. "You don't mind being different?" Christabel minded her unfashionable auburn hair dreadfully.

"I take it as a gift from the Great Mother. Her hand touches me. It is a good omen for my people. I have the medicine way. So I must tell you that when you get home, you should drink as much hot liquid as you can. Ask your mother for tea made with the mustard leaf."

Christabel seriously doubted her mother would have mustard leaf and if she did that she would make tea with it. But she couldn't tell Rahdonee that. She'd think they were backward or something. "I know my way from here," she said instead. "I'm not afraid anymore."

Rahdonee stopped. "Are you certain?" She nodded vigorously, even though she was a little scared of getting caught on her way in through the millpond. "I don't know...thank you for..."

"Thank the Great Mother," Rahdonee said, solemnly. Then her eyes sparkled and she held out one hand. "I am so pleased to have met you. I hope we shall meet again."

Christabel snickered and shook Rahdonee's hand. She imitated Reverend Downing's wife very well indeed. "Likewise, I'm sure."

"We shall meet again," Rahdonee called over her shoulder. She loped into the darkness, and Christabel turned toward home.

She made good on her plan to say she got muddy going to the church. The sky was lightening, and those few people up that early could not see her well enough to tell she was soaked and muddy. She slipped into the church and found it empty, as she had hoped.

It was only slightly warmer inside than out, and she huddled on a back pew, wishing for her bed and the tea Rahdonee suggested. Thinking of Rahdonee made her look around the church with new eyes. Its simplicity was a tenet of the Puritan faith. There were no gold chalices or fancy altar linens to incur the wrath of God over pagan idols. She had never been particularly touched by the church, except when Reverend Downing's wife read *Pilgrim's Progress* aloud in Sunday school. She had had a voice much prettier than her looks and Christabel had liked her for her warm, melodic voice. She missed the Downings.

She didn't like Reverend Gorony. She supposed she ought to, but he frightened her. He was so angry all the time. And he wouldn't let her read anymore. She thought maybe Pa was afraid of him, too, and realizing that Pa could be afraid of anyone had made her dislike the new Reverend all the more.

She ran her hand over the rough-hewn wood of the pew, then slipped into the aisle and approached the altar. It was equally rough, but she liked the smell of it. Rahdonee said the Great Mother was Christ's mother. She would have to think about that. Rahdonee said that the Great Mother was in the trees and rain and stars. She touched the altar appreciatively. That meant the Great Mother was here.

That was a comforting thought.

In the future when she came here she would think about Rahdonee and the Great Mother. It would help pass the time.

When she judged it to be past rising at the Albright's, she peeked out the church door. There didn't appear to be anyone there, so she slipped out, planning to wait for someone to appear at the end of the street to witness her fall from the sidewalk into the muck.

She had just made it to the edge of the walk when a voice grated in her ear.

"What have you been doing in God's house?"

She yelped and backed away from Reverend Gorony's outraged gaze. He reached for her. She lost her footing and tumbled backward into the mire.

There was an outcry of several voices, and then people were all around her, lifting her up. She was filthy right to her hair. She wiped mud off her brow, protesting that she was fine. Only then did she dare look up at the preacher.

He was very angry. She didn't know if he'd got a good enough look at her to know she had been dirty before she fell.

Well, he was looking at her now. Her cloak was still in the mud, and her dress clung to her like a second skin.

It was Mr. Dennison who helped her back up onto the sidewalk and wrapped her cloak around her. The cloak didn't provide any warmth at all, but she felt protected. Reverend Gorony was still staring at her.

"What were you doing in church?"

It was harder to lie with Mr. Dennison listening, too. "I, I wanted to pray, so I got up very early and, and when I was done I felt better and I was going to go home again so my folks wouldn't miss me. I didn't want anyone to know." She was thinking as fast as she could—demonstrations of excessive piety were almost as bad as no piety at all.

Reverend Gorony's expression had changed, but he was still angry—and suspicious. "You are too old to be on the street so early by yourself."

Mr. Dennison agreed. "Chrissy, you should be home safe and sound. There could be tavern folk still about. I'll walk you home."

She turned gratefully toward home, but looked back over her shoulder when Reverend Gorony spoke.

"I want you to come see me before Sunday. We need to discuss your sudden need for prayer."

Christabel gulped. He suspected her of being up to something, but didn't know what. She'd have to figure out the best things to say that wouldn't get her in more trouble.

Mr. Dennison left her at their gate, and Christabel thanked him for his trouble. She knew he'd tell Goody Dennison about it, then their daughter, Martha, would tell Bitsy—she and Bitsy were thick as thieves sometimes. Well, that was fine. Bitsy would know she'd slept under the tree then. But knowing she'd nearly died took some of the satisfaction out of it.

Smoke was curling in the chimney, which meant Ma was up. Her mother turned from the fire when the door opened.

"Chrissy!"

"Ma, I fell. I went to the church to pray—" She got no more out of her mouth before her mother slapped her, and then began stripping her of the filthy clothes.

"I've never seen such a child—how could you embarrass your pa like this? The Reverend saw you? What were you thinking, child? You're too old for this."

Christabel was dizzy by the time Ma finished pulling off the clothes. She had expected to get slapped; she was used to it.

"There's no time to boil water and I won't have you messing up a blanket." Ma was hauling the heavy steel bath into the center of the wet porch. "If your father sees you like this there'll be plenty to pay, I can tell you."

With a shudder, Christabel realized what was coming. Ma lifted one of the buckets of water from in front of the fire and poured it into the bath. "In you go, girl. I don't want any arguments from you."

She stepped gingerly into the cold water and sat shivering. The water had been slightly warmed, but not enough. Ma came back from the pump and tipped the bucket over her head. The shock of the icy water made her cry out, and all the cold and misery when Rahdonee found her flooded back.

"Stop your whining, girl. You reap what you sow." She stomped down the steps to the pump again.

Christabel tried to put the soap to good use while Ma was gone, hoping the water would hide her tears. Another bucket of water made her shiver uncontrollably.

"You brought this on yourself. I don't have time to heat water."

She'd made a lot of extra work for Ma. That was for certain. She'd be lucky to escape a whipping.

Ma didn't whip her, and neither did Pa, though that might have been because he had to meet Lord Berkeley by mid-morning for an overnight trip to the mainland. She spent the day scrubbing pots on the wet porch and then plucking the quail Pa had brought home last evening. Even her own bed, with wrapped hot bricks at her feet, didn't make her warm.

By the next morning she was feverish, and it had started to rain again.

Chapter 5

"Dina! How delightful you could take the time to meet us." Leonard Goranson greeted Dina like a long lost friend. They'd exchanged two phone calls and several e-mails in the last two days, and his effusiveness felt false to her. She stiffened as he kissed her cheeks, European style, and fought the urge to brush her face and arms where he'd touched her.

"It's a luxury," Dina said carefully. She hardly wanted to encourage him to think she could drop everything in the evenings and continue acting as tour guide.

Then Christa emerged from the cab as well and Dina knew she'd never resent any situation that let them spend time together. Her body's reaction to Christa's two quick kisses on her cheeks was markedly different.

She forgot what she was going to say when she realized Goranson was watching them speculatively and whatever it was he saw pleased him. The look in his eyes was unclean, like he was imagining her and Christa performing sex acts just for him. She fought back another shudder. She would not let him make her feel soiled.

Looking carefully blank, Christa said, "We hardly had time

the other night to see that one floor. I mentioned to Leo what a good guide you were. You're so kind to go back so soon."

Dina gave Christa a reassuring smile. "It's no bother."

Goranson's phone chirped.

He stepped a few feet away, spoke quickly and even before he hung up Dina knew he was going to beg off. She felt strongly that the call was prearranged, and her certainty had nothing to do with any gift from her mother. All he had cared about was that she and Christa spent more time together, and that should worry her.

"One of the girls is having a bad shoot," he said, already flagging a cab. "I was deluding myself thinking I could skip it."

"What a shame." Even to her own ears, Dina knew she sounded unconvincing.

"You two enjoy yourselves." A cab pulled to the curb and just like that he was gone. Fortunately, Dina thought, he took his slime factor with him.

"Are you sure you're not tired?" Dina glanced down at the very narrow, toe-pinching shoes Christa wore. It was easier to look at her shoes than her face. Forty-eight hours had not dimmed the memory of those amazing eyes.

"I'm fine. Please don't worry about me." Christa turned toward the museum's entrance, her step light and quick. "I apologize for Leo, though."

"I understand that things come up." Goranson's entire attitude ought to have made her wary, but Christa's nearness was too unsettling—and welcome—to worry about Goranson's motives. "We don't have to go the museum again."

"Please." Christa's smile was almost shy. "We didn't finish the other night and I'd like to see more. Unless you're tired."

Dina wasn't in the least bit tired now—wandering through MOMA always picked up her spirits, and tonight would be no different even if her body was behaving irrationally. Yes, she told herself crossly, Christa is very beautiful and I don't have to turn into a babbling lump of neediness because of it. "In that case, I think you should see the Mary Cassatts next."

"I'd love that." She gave Dina a brilliant smile that seemed to drive back the light drizzle. Heads turned and Dina prayed she didn't look as dazzled as she felt. This second outing might still have been at Goranson's instigation, but clearly Christa wasn't unwilling. Dina sternly quelled her body's imaginative conjectures.

It was easier to forget her very adult reactions to Christa when Christa's sophistication melted away. She confessed she was looking at her first Picasso, her first Cassatt, her first Warhol. Christa actually gasped and clapped her hands when she saw the twenty-five-foot high Oldenburg soft sculpture. The giant pillow was just the beginning, and Dina let Christa take her time with each new artwork, trying to sort out how an exterior so sophisticated, blasé even, could hide a childlike enthusiasm for vivid colors and rich textures.

This is dangerous, she thought. Christa wasn't just desirable, she was someone Dina could like. More than like. Interesting, intelligent…dangerous. Her experiences with relationships in the past, none deep or successful, told her to keep some distance. Part of her knew it was too late. When that intuitive gift ought to have warned caution too, curiously, Dina felt as if an inner voice was telling her *not* to hold back.

They moved from room to room while Dina wrestled with her inner conflicts. Christa saw paintings in their component pieces of light and color—watching Christa respond on an almost purely emotional level to modern art left Dina feeling as if she might be able to understand it herself. She was no longer certain which of them was the guide.

"Have you thought about painting or sculpting?"

Christa shook her head. "Just because I appreciate art doesn't make me an artist. I don't really have time. Time for that kind of extensive study, I mean."

Dina could understand that. "What about fashion design? You've just shown me more about the light and shadow in that Frankenthaler than I've ever seen before. Textiles, as I've learned in the past two days, are art for the body."

Christa's expression took on shadows. "I don't have time for that either."

Dina was distracted from the thought that they each meant something different by *time* when the first warning of closing time was announced. Christa's heartfelt plea to the security guard bought them an extra fifteen minutes. What must it be like, Dina thought, to have that kind of power over men?

And not just men, she had to admit. Women's heads turned as well, though some with resentment. Some, like her, seemed bemused. Christa didn't seem to notice any of it. Her focus was on the art. Dina watched the way Christa's warm amber eyes drank in textures, shapes and colors. They were full of dancing light, remarkably changed from the dark mist Dina had first seen in them. Each time Dina made eye contact with Christa she swore she heard the soft chime of bells. Ridiculous, she told herself. Pretty eyes—since when did she get all disturbed by a pair of pretty eyes?

It wasn't just the eyes, her body answered. The rest of Christa was deeply disturbing, too. She was only a few inches shorter than Dina. Just the right height, in fact. She was as generously made as Marilyn Monroe, including the slight swelling of her belly and round, full hips. Long, slim legs gave way to an inviting curve of thigh that made Dina catch her breath. All of that was perfectly discernible under a modest, cowl-necked gold-flecked sweater of deep burgundy over black slacks that clung in the right places. In a swimsuit...the image didn't bear thinking about. And yet with no difficulty at all, Dina could picture Christa's hair spread on a pillow of leaves and could imagine the warmth of her stomach under her cheek.

Such imaginings were utterly pointless and unproductive—and vividly arousing.

It was easy to get a table at Armanio's at that late hour. Dina noticed that Christa's cheeks flushed as she inhaled a plate of capellini with scallops.

Her own salmon and fettuccine Alfredo was a frightful indulgence, but at least she could tell Jeff she had had a substantial dinner.

"This must be what ambrosia tastes like." Christa sopped up the last of her marinara sauce with her focaccia.

"What do you normally eat? Melba toast and yogurt?"

"Gack, not me. I just didn't get any lunch." She made a face. "Leo likes my figure just the way it is. I don't have to starve myself, just exercise for tone."

"That's not too bad. I thought all models had to starve themselves."

"Most do. You can't exercise too much or you'll get muscles, heaven forbid. It wouldn't be a bad life at all, except..."

"Except what?" Christa's eyes had gone smoky again.

"Never mind. Not tonight, anyway." She gave her full attention to wiping her fingers on her napkin.

"I enjoyed the museum," Dina said. "I don't go often enough."

"What's your excuse? Too much work?"

"Too much work. I sometimes go weeks with the cell phone implanted in my ear."

"Why do you do it? All those hours?"

Dina was caught off guard. "That's a very good question. One I don't ask myself often enough."

"That's not an answer." Christa sipped from her wine. Her lips were the color of the Shiraz, and Dina had to admit to herself that kissing those lips was very much on her mind.

Fumbling to hide her distraction, she countered with, "Why do you do your work?" Dina expected something along the lines of "Because I can."

"Escape."

"As good a reason as any," Dina said. She realized it was very close to her own reasons for working ninety hours a week. "Escape from where? Or what?"

Christa took a long time to answer. "Mostly from where I grew up. How I grew up. I thought Leo was an escape from that. Well, truthfully, he was."

Dina's skin crawled as an unbidden image of Goranson with

Christa tortured her mind. Her stomach turned, and she had to swallow hard. "And now?"

The Christa who had laughed at the soft sculpture was gone. "You think I still need to escape?"

"Doesn't matter what I think. What do you think?"

"That you're a lousy therapist." Dina hated Christa's taunting smile. It reminded her too much of Goranson. Goranson with Christa—the image literally nauseated Dina.

The waiter's arrival with the check was fortuitous. Dina struggled to keep her dinner down, hoping she had the flu and not, well, she just hoped it was the flu. She needed some breathing space from Christa...and Goranson.

Christa paid the check before Dina realized what was happening. "That wasn't necessary," she said.

"I know. But this way you'll have to pay next time."

Next time. The phrase hung in the air between them, and Dina knew there would be a next time. She knew her own reasons, but not Christa's. Or rather, she didn't want to face Christa's reasons because Leonard Goranson was behind them, lurking in the darkness that had returned to Christa's eyes.

"How was your date?"

I wanted to say it had not been a date. Leo was only provoking me. I didn't want to talk to him at all, but he gestured at the chair across from him with his most smug expression.

"I've been thinking about our arrangement," he said without any further formalities. His smile faded when I didn't answer. "You'll be on the July cover of *Vogue*."

I knew he expected me to be happy. My picture on the cover of at least six major magazines was what I figured would make me immortal. No matter what happened to me, someone would remember that I had been here. Given the history of women in my family, it was a goal I never thought I'd achieve. At least until Leo came along.

Leo had promised me my immortality. *Cosmopolitan* and now *Vogue* were in line, four more to go. "When did you find out?"

He was annoyed at my lack of reaction. "Several days ago. I thought I'd save the news for a special occasion."

"Is this a special occasion?"

"It could be." He looked me up and down and I broke out in goose bumps, chilled to the pit of my stomach.

"If I'm going to be doing photo shoots, not to mention runway walks when you unveil here, I can't be pregnant."

"I'd design a line of maternity wear just for you."

I swallowed hard. "You still have to get me four more magazines."

"It's only a matter of time, my dear." He was leaning over my chair now. His fingers grazed my cheek. I steeled myself not to flinch. "Why wait?"

"When you keep your end of the arrangement, I'll keep mine."

He dropped his hands to my shoulders, and I couldn't hold back my shudders anymore. He didn't move his hands. His anger was singeing my skin. "Will you? You'll be willing? You'll have to work much, much harder on your acting."

I tore myself out from under his hands and faced him, unsteady on my feet. That I go willingly to his bed was his reward for my immortality. I supposed I should be grateful he didn't force me, but for some reason, he insisted I be willing. All of the women who went to him were willing, at least at the beginning. I didn't want to remember some of their faces, gone almost before they'd arrived, thinking Leo would expend the same effort on them he spent on me. There were a few, like Liza Brightly, who had the talent and the nature to please Leo personally and professionally. That she was the queen of his bedroom was something she never let me forget. She didn't understand how little I cared.

I knew I never would be willing to sleep with him, to do what Liza was willing to do. But I could see in his eyes that he believed that some day I would. He believed he could twist me, make me something I'm not. And what Leonard believed was possible often turned out to be.

"So you enjoyed your evening with Ms. Financial Wizard?"

"It was okay." He laughed as if he hadn't heard anything so amusing in months. I thought of Dina's light, how it warmed me and let me see clearly for the first time in years.

"Pity we're leaving so soon. I'll have to think of a way to arrange another date for you two. I'm certain Dina enjoyed herself."

I turned my face away, knowing the angle made it a little harder for him to read my thoughts. "I'm very tired. I'd like to go to my room."

"Of course. We're having lunch tomorrow with the fashion editor from *Vogue*. You'll need to look well-rested."

I slipped my shoes off and tried to move as if I weren't longing to run.

"Oh, yes. Christa, my love."

I paused but did not look at him.

"When she gets you into bed, you *will* let me know, won't you?"

I didn't answer, and his pleased laugh followed me into my room. I closed the door with a calm click and dropped to the floor, too spent to move another step.

He'd had me turn on the charm to close deals before. Not innocent, certainly, but somewhat a part of the business game. For millennia, men had used women to make other men irrational. I was not in any position to think I was any different from women probably much smarter and much stronger than I would ever be.

The air was stale, and I felt sticky and trapped. A fly in a spider web. The spider wasn't going to eat me—not yet. I was just bait for other flies.

But Dina was different. He didn't want just money, or just contacts, or just information. He wanted Dina. He desired her light. When she wanted me—not when, I knew she already did—he would use that to bend her to his plans. He would consume her light and cast her aside, just as he would cast me aside once I'd given him the child he required. We were sport to him, and nothing more.

How did I get here? Nothing was like I had thought it would be. I'd known Leo was no saint, but I hadn't expected him to be a devil, either. I didn't want to be party to delivering Dina up to his darkness. And yet I was already craving the warmth of her presence again.

If I had a high road open to me I couldn't see it. The women in my family are not strong enough, and don't live long enough, to make good choices. And I have no reason to think I am any different.

"I don't feel so good, Ma, really."

Her mother's hand drifted over her forehead. "Well, I wouldn't be surprised if you haven't gone and caught yourself a cold. I'll make some comfit."

With a sinking feeling Christabel watched her mother prepare a cup of her cure-all for everything from chilblain to runny nose. It was vile stuff, almost worse than being sick. She held her nose and drank it down. She wondered if Rahdonee's mustard leaf tea tasted better.

It may have been the very meekness with which she drank the comfit that made her mother stroke her forehead more gently and say, "If you don't feel better by supper, I'll get the doctor."

The doctor was very expensive. Bitsy said that he'd bled Bitsy's brother when he had a dog bite and that had saved his life. Christabel swallowed hard at the idea of being bled, and she thought even more longingly of Rahdonee's mustard leaf tea.

"I'll get better, Ma, I'm sure. It's just the cold and the rain."

"I'm sure you'll be fine. Put down the sewing and come sit by the hearth."

She was actually feeling better. Sort of light-headed and distant, but better. Except for the ache in her neck, and, well, she ached all over. But that was really not that important because all at once it seemed like the aches belonged to someone else.

When she woke, she heard her father's voice and was comforted by it.

"You were right to send for the doctor," he was saying.

"I should have done it yesterday right off when she said she couldn't get warm. But I was so mad at her."

"Don't fret—she's very strong."

"I know." It sounded like Ma was close by, but even close by was a long way off. "I keep thinking about the Cornwall boys."

Dickie and George Cornwall had died last summer from a fever that wouldn't break, leaving their parents childless. *Am I going to die?* She was an only child. Ma wouldn't have anyone to help make butter this summer. She frowned and then decided the matter concerned someone else.

A sharp pain in her arm told her the doctor was there, but she had no need to look. It was someone else's arm, anyway. Rahdonee's tree spirits were singing more beautifully than any choir ever could. They sang for about a year, then until tomorrow, and she heard Reverend Gorony's voice. She listened because she wanted to make sure he didn't tell Ma that she'd been fibbing about going to pray.

"She must cast out all wickedness, all presence of the devil."

That was nonsense. She didn't believe in Satan. Uh-oh. That was blasphemy. Better not think about it.

"She hasn't opened her eyes for a day. How can she cast out anything?" Ma sounded really unhappy. She wanted to tell Ma not to worry, that she was going to be fine.

"We must help her with prayer. The devil cannot have her. Say it with me. The Lord is my shepherd..."

Of course the devil couldn't have her. The low murmur of voices was distracting, but after a while she didn't hear them anymore.

The lamps were bright, or it was day, or she was under a blanket of fog. Her forehead was wet; there was water in her eyes. She blinked it away and tried to ask where Ma was. Then she heard Ma's voice.

"I don't know what I'm going to do, Lizzy." Ma was sure upset about something. Her voice was all funny, thick and raspy.

"Let me pray for a while, Edith," Goody Dennison was nice.

It was good she was helping Ma. "You should get some sleep or you'll sicken yourself."

"I can't sleep. She's my only baby. I have to ask you something. Do you think that this might be a native sickness? Maybe one of the native women—I've heard it said they have their own medicines."

"Put it from your mind." Goody Dennison sounded shocked. "You know that's just the devil's mischief. They're godless and unclean."

"Not all. Some have come to the church."

"If they have truly accepted the Lord, then they've put all that pagan witchery behind them. Put it from your mind."

"I can't. She's my only baby."

The water on her forehead was distracting her again. The lamps dimmed, and she heard Pa's voice. It was easier to sleep when he was near.

Her bed jolted and she could almost open her eyes. Someone was shouting. Pa. Ma, too. Ma was crying, and then she heard Reverend Gorony again. He was making Ma cry, the cur.

"If she lives, then we'll worry about getting her soul back from the devil." Pa was using his officer voice, and she marveled that Reverend Gorony wasn't silent and at attention.

"Her immortal soul is more important than the vessel of flesh. We cannot give it to witches and demons for healing and then expect them to give it back."

"I'll march to hell itself to get it back, Reverend."

"You're treading dangerous ground. I forbid this."

There was a silence so heavy that Christabel felt it bearing down on her chest. She couldn't breathe.

Ma was holding her up all of a sudden, and the ache eased. "Please," she was crying. "The devil can have my soul. I'd give it to him gladly for her to be well again!"

Ma, Christabel thought, you shouldn't say things like that. What if they came true?

"Blasphemer! Your thoughts have already delivered you to the devil!"

"Best you leave now, Reverend." Pa's voice was low, but fierce. "Leave before I forget you're a man of God."

It was quiet. Christabel was only aware of her mother rocking her. Then there was the gentle ha-woofing sound the mare made when she was being saddled, followed by the muffled beat of hooves disappearing into the fog.

Chapter 6

Jason Williams put up his umbrella as he and Dina emerged into the early evening. "I can't believe it's still raining."

Glad to be out of the future home of LGI's North American "gallery," Dina hoped her tone was more assured than she felt. "I'm starting to wish I had webbed feet. Look at the traffic." An accident, the rain—whatever the cause, cars were at a dead stop on both Fifty-fifth and Fifth Avenue. Peering through the rain, Dina thought Sixth Avenue didn't look any more promising.

"I think we may have to settle for the subway." The construction engineer held his umbrella over both of them.

"You're right. There's no way a cab is moving in this." Every step from the building she felt better but there were still shivers running like electric current across her shoulders. She hated the place, which was ridiculous.

"We could get a bite to eat. I know a little place with sweet potato fries around the corner."

"Just like mama used to make?" Dina had grown to like and trust Jason during their meetings to go over the construction estimates. Having him inside the building with her was comforting, and his practical manner was welcome when her own psyche was being so odd.

"Hardly. Mama pan fried potatoes in bacon grease."

"Bet they were delicious." At the moment, with her nerves all over the place, Dina felt queasy at the thought.

"That they were. I'd give a lot for a plate right now."

They turned onto Fifth as Dina said, "My mother made kitchen sink soup. Somehow it was always delicious no matter what got put into it. A bowl of that would be welcome when I get home." Now that was true, she realized. A steaming bowl of soup and a talk with her mother would be comforting beyond words. The former was unlikely, given the contents of her cupboards, and she didn't believe in any of the methods that would supposedly allow the latter. Yet she knew her mother would have helped her figure out why that building—and Christa—had gotten under her skin.

Jason gave a casual parting wave. "I'll get the revised estimates over by the end of the week."

Dina waved back and pushed her way into the crowd for the next uptown train. Usually she didn't like crowds but tonight, after the inevitable chill she got from being in that building, the warmth was welcome. It didn't matter that Goranson and Christa had left town two weeks ago—the building made her hands go cold.

Jostling for position near a strap, she just managed to grab hold before the train moved. Her arms ached and maybe, finally, after feeling so unlike herself for weeks now, she really was catching the flu.

The train wasn't that crowded but she felt pushed on from all sides. People were talking loudly—that's what she thought at first. But then, glancing around, she saw that most were silent, looking as tired as she felt. There was still a lot of noise, though, as if Dina could hear the babble of all those weary thoughts.

Bricks, she thought. Build a wall of bricks. It was an old trick her mother had taught her as a child, making a game out of a basic calming technique. She started with the first row of big, thick bricks only to lose her mental grip on the image and start over again when they pulled into the next station.

After a few minutes she realized her gaze had settled on a middle-aged woman across the train from her. Her suit said she was probably in middle management, and the neatly wrapped dreads framed a troubled expression. I don't want to know, Dina thought, I don't want—she fumbled the bricks and started again.

They pulled into Dina's stop and she made her way off the train, biting her tongue hard to keep from saying, as she passed the woman, "Say yes. It'll be okay."

It was one thing to have these insane flashes of whatever-the-hell they were, but quite another to actually say them. She was not about to become the crazy lady nobody would make eye contact with.

Soaked by the rain as she walked from the subway to her apartment building, Dina half hoped she did have the flu. Her energy supply was depleted and it was hard work fighting off feelings she didn't want to have. Long hours, she told herself, it's just long hours and too many little details.

She closed her own door behind her and gave up the bricks, letting them turn to water. The day's held-back impressions and the kept-out intuitions, they all flooded in, soaking her senses with the helpless horror she had felt all around her in Leonard Goranson's building. She fumbled her way to the nearest chair and let them all come. Inevitably, her thoughts also turned to Christa.

Christa's smile and bright eyes were crowded out of her mind by a vision of Goranson. His personal darkness blotted out everything for a minute, leaving Dina gasping. She slammed her mental bricks back into place as the darkness began to drain her—it was like nothing she had ever felt.

She opened her eyes sometime later and recalled the number of times she had seen her mother in this state. Thanks, Mom, Dina thought. This isn't something I wanted to inherit. Some "gift." She hadn't signed up for crazy impulses to talk to strangers and feeling creeped out just because some designer guy is a jerk.

She didn't have her mother's saintly patience, her depthless compassion for others and unending empathy for anyone in pain. There was no way she could inherit the gift—or curse, depending on your point of view. These episodes of feeling overwhelmed were the result of overwork and poor eating habits. When she made partner, she would completely change her life.

There, she thought, that was settled. Just a little while longer and she would get a life.

She downed three Advil tablets and drank half a quart of milk. She had intended to take a long, hot bath, but instead she folded her clothes in the laundry and dry-cleaning hampers for Pedra and tumbled into bed.

She slipped into the dream before she knew she was asleep. A great cavern opened before her, and she hovered unseen amid stalactites that dripped viscous lemon-lime liquid. The dank smell of rotting peat and trapped water overwhelmed her, and she struggled to stop gagging.

She became aware of chittering below her. She moved slightly, and drew back in horror. The clicks and mutters came from a hunched demon, a creature of nightmare, encrusted in black, oily muck out of which stared feral, red eyes. It gibbered and cackled as it snatched something out of the air, devouring whatever it was in a single gulp.

She didn't want to get closer, but she was slowly drifting downward. She saw a minute flash of silver light, then the demon snatched it out of the air and gobbled it up. Threads—they were like small strands of thread. The brighter in color, the happier the creature seemed. It was feeding steadily, but Dina could sense its hunger growing with every swallow. There would never be enough to satisfy this hunger.

The demon gave a sudden yowl of frustration. Momentarily, there were no more threads. It scrabbled across the cavern floor to a twisted and chewed coil of thick, reddish strings and fed on it briefly. Dina sensed it held itself back from eating too much, as if this was the only guaranteed food and must be devoured only at utmost need.

At the moment she realized she could understand the creature's primal thoughts, the hunched figure looked up, right into her eyes. All in an instant it bared its teeth and launched itself upward, talons extended.

Her own scream terrified her more than the demon's attack. She tried to move but was nightmare frozen as the razored claws reached for her throat—only to rebound on the barrier between her nightmare and its reality. It howled in frustration, and the cavern dissolved like a chalk painting in the rain.

She had no sensation of waking from the nightmare. Her eyes were open as if she had never slept. The dreamcatcher that had been her mother's was rocking on the wall as if from a light breeze. Her only proof that time had even passed was the sweat-drenched sheets.

The thud of hoofbeats approaching brought Rahdonee to her feet along with most of the others who sat enjoying the early evening fire. She did not recognize the Englishman or the horse, but he rode as if he carried a heavy burden and was in great haste.

She fetched her bodeb from her tent and was already walking toward the man when Sinhaya beckoned to her. Sinhaya had learned the language of the Dutch, but struggled with the English.

"How can we help you?" Rahdonee studied the man as he assessed her. A soldier, it was unmistakable. If he was startled at being addressed by a young female, he didn't show it. Yet his face was clearly lined with tension.

"My daughter is ill. A fever that began two days ago. We have heard you had medicines."

"I am the medicine keeper. My medicines are not welcome in your town. By some."

"I will protect you with my own life, if necessary." The mare shuffled on the cold ground, and the soldier brought her effortlessly under control. "We are desperate. No matter what"—he stopped to swallow—"we will be generous to you for coming."

Her mind flashed with the image of young Christabel, and she accepted the Great Mother's prompting. If it was Christabel, then she had to complete the duty the Great Mother had sent to her. She struck her bargain.

"Our pigs sickened after harvest. The sickness was in your town as well. We need stock to start again."

"Done," he said. "Have you a horse?"

"No. Will your horse carry two?"

He offered a hand to pull her up in front of him, but she shook her head. "It will be faster if I go behind. What is your name and house place?" She repeated the answers to Sinhaya, should he want to find her, and accepted Sinhaya's cupped hands onto the horse's back. He handed up her cloak, and she wrapped her arms around the man's waist.

"I can stay on," she told him. "Ride at your best speed." The words had barely left her mouth when he wheeled his gallant mare into the forest.

"It's been all day since she has wet." Ma's voice came from a great distance. All the way from England, maybe. Christabel opened her eyes and peered down a long, dark tunnel. There were people at the other end, but they were not looking at her.

"We must make her drink—"

"She must be bled!"

"No." The new voice was firm, but gentle. Familiar. "Liquids to replace what you have taken. Water to make her body work."

"Doctor? How can tea hurt her?"

"It can't, I suppose, but she must be bled soon."

"No. Tea from these leaves." A dark-haired woman handed something to Ma. "I can make her drink." After a moment she added, "Do not worry, I think it is not too late."

Ma left, but Christabel could hear her crying. She'd been such a bother to Ma these last few days.

The dark-haired woman was leaning toward her—it was

Rahdonee. Christabel wanted to jump for joy, but couldn't manage even a smile. Suddenly the tunnel threatened to collapse, leaving her lost on the other side, but even as darkness closed in, it seemed as if a bolt of pure green light flooded into Christabel's mind and pulled her to Rahdonee's side of the tunnel.

A voice clearly said, right inside her head, "You are not going yet."

When Ma brought the tea she tried to cooperate and swallow, but she didn't blame Rahdonee for having to pinch her nose and jab her in the ribs. The tea was kind of tingly going down.

"I don't know if we'll ever get her hair unmatted," Ma said. "Maybe I should cut it."

"We'll work it out together," Rahdonee said. Her voice was lovely, Christabel remembered. Like bells from a distant hillside. "I will need to stay for a day or two."

"Is she really going to be right again?"

"I believe so. I will sit with her tonight. You need to sleep or you will not be useful to her tomorrow."

"I can't," Ma said.

"You can." Rahdonee touched Ma's cheek gently. "Sleep for a while. I will wake you if anything changes."

Christabel was vastly relieved when Ma left. Ma needed her sleep. Rahdonee was like a warm blanket of caring. She was saying something in her own language. The cadence was like prayer.

Christabel let the darkness come back, but this time it was sleep and not oblivion.

When she next woke it was to drink more tea. She found she could help a little. After, Rahdonee cleaned her face and hands, and slipped clean sheets under and over her. It felt heavenly.

She woke at the cock's crow, aware of where she was and no longer feeling far away. A quiet noise made her turn her head. Rahdonee was rising out of Ma's chair and smiling at her. Her long, brilliant hair was tied back, and she looked so...pure in her simple buckskin dress.

"You are back, aren't you?"

"I feel like it," Christabel managed to croak. "I've been so much trouble to you and Ma now."

"Yes. But you will do better in the future."

Christabel liked her for not saying it was no bother. Bitsy's mother was always saying things were no bother when they obviously were. "I'm hungry."

Rahdonee grinned. "I'll tell your mother. She has been baking something from the moment she woke."

The something turned out to be Christabel's favorite skillet cake, with lots of oats and butter and some of the precious brown spice from India. A while after that, Ma's eggs and rashers of bacon were very welcome indeed.

She ate, slept, and then felt well enough to toilet herself, not shy at all when Rahdonee helped her into a fresh dressing gown. After all, Rahdonee had seen her unclothed once already. She was settling into sleep when Pa knocked on the door.

He spoke first to Rahdonee. "I've sent the stockman up the island with a pregnant sow and three one-year-olds. One of them is a male from a different litter."

"Thank you," Rahdonee said. "That is more than generous."

"It's not enough," Pa answered. He sounded gruff. Then he cleared his throat and smiled down at me.

"You'll need to rest up a few days, I imagine." He put a book on the coverlet.

Christabel touched the cover. It was the book of myths that he'd taken back because Reverend Gorony said women didn't need to read such things. "Thanks, Pa. I've been a lot of bother."

"That you have," Pa said, but I could tell he wasn't angry. He glanced at Rahdonee. "You should thank this girl, though. She brought her own medicines for you."

She almost said that she already knew Rahdonee, but remembered just in time. "I will, Pa."

Pa started to say something, but snapped around to the doorway in response to a sharp, prolonged knock on the front door. Ma was first subdued, then more agitated.

Reverend Gorony burst into the room, and Christabel clutched Pa's book to her, suddenly deeply afraid. Pa stood in his way. Then Rahdonee also stepped between the Reverend and her.

"You have brought the devil's tool into your home! I warned you of the consequences."

"Reverend, I am a Christian woman," Rahdonee said, carefully. "I was saved by Reverend Downing."

"Christian? Eve in disguise. You wear your temptations like a common strumpet, your harlot legs exposed—"

Christabel never forgot what happened next. Pa lifted Reverend Gorony up with one hand around his neck, right up off his feet. "You'll not damage my honor, *sir*."

Reverend Gorony clawed at Pa's hand, but Pa shook him like a puppy. "This is Goodwoman Geraldine, a Christian Manhattan woman, and an honored guest in my house. I am sure you are delighted to make her acquaintance." Pa let the choking man drop back to his feet.

Rahdonee said, "Delighted to meet you, I'm sure."

Christabel had a fit of weak giggles, but swallowed them when Reverend Gorony glared at her. He looked down at her dressing gown, and Christabel felt ashamed to be undressed in front of him. She pulled the coverlet up to her chin, but she could still feel the pressure of his eyes.

But she wasn't relieved when his gazed turned to Rahdonee. He looked at her with eyes of fire. Rahdonee met his fierce gaze, and Christabel marveled that she showed no signs of fear, only a firm constancy. As if she would always be there, had always been there, facing him.

Reverend Gorony glared at Pa, his face twisting. Then he stormed out of the room and subsequently the house.

"The priest begat unbelief," Pa muttered.

"And unbelief begat rage," Rahdonee added, but Pa didn't hear her.

Chapter 7

"Just one more, Bella! One more!"

I ached from my hips down, and if ever I had wanted out of my shoes it was now. This was supposed to be a cocktail party, and we were still in the lobby of the London Windsor Hotel, surrounded by paparazzi. Leo had no intention of shooing them away. All publicity was good publicity, he said, as long as they mentioned my LG designer apparel.

Elle magazine was hosting the party, ostensibly to thank supporters of a charity event they'd hosted, but really to give advertisers a chance to press the flesh with celebrities. I didn't think I fit in that category, and the press's interest in me had caught me off guard.

Of course it could have been the cleavage. Leo had left very little to anyone's imagination. The strapless bra was stabbing my underarms as it relentlessly pushed down on my stomach.

I couldn't smile anymore. "Leo, the shoes are the wrong size. I think they're Liza's, not mine. I'm going to limp for a week."

"A few more," he said.

The electric-blue cocktail sheath had been designed exclusively for me and I knew that hundreds of women would count themselves lucky to be squeezed, pinched, prodded and taped into it for a few hours. It was far less comfortable than the clothes Leo would be rolling out in New York. The bodice was cut so low I felt indecent, which was silly. Women had been taking their tops off to be rich and famous for, well, forever. My body was my passport to immortality, but tonight was turning out to be one of the occasions when I didn't like what it did to everybody around me and the damned clothes just plain hurt.

The clamor didn't end. "Bella, could you bend over a little? One more! One more!"

I straightened my spine. I hated that the photographers called me Bella, as if I was some Italian trollop, and I was not going to drop to all fours à la Marilyn Monroe to give them their cheap thrill. I wanted immortality, but if I had wanted it for being a sex symbol I would have stayed in Hollywood.

I wanted to be remembered for my face and my *full* name, not my breasts. I had my mother's face, and her mother's face, and if I could make the world remember me, it would seem as if they were remembered, too. That all the women in my family weren't pathetic drones, used up before they turned thirty.

"It's time to go, boys," Leo announced. "La Christabel has been very accommodating."

He twirled me toward the elevator, a graceful move he liked. It photographed well. But before I knew it, I was in his arms and he was dipping me, ballroom style.

The next thing I knew I was looking at the bank of photographers upside down.

Leo pulled me upright again. I stumbled into the elevator, blinded from the flashbulbs. Of course it had been deliberate. I wouldn't cooperate, so Leo had practically dropped me on my back so the whole world could take a good, long look down my dress.

I swung at him before I knew what I was doing, but he easily caught my arm, and then deftly twisted it. My fingers went numb.

"Don't give yourself airs, darling. They'll put your face on the cover, but all they really want"—he shoved his hand up my skirt, and the sheer pantyhose I wore was no protection from his fingers—"is this."

He let go of me so suddenly that I fell. He yanked me back to my feet as the elevator doors opened.

"Smile," he hissed.

"I need the bathroom." It was the only place he couldn't follow me—at least not without making the kind of scene he loathed.

"Fine. Get some color in those cheeks. You look like a ghost."

I sat in a stall, feeling as if I was going to throw up. Once upon a time I had thought that what movie producers, theatrical agents and casting managers wanted me to do both with them and on film was dirty. That it would make me feel soiled and used, and it would set me on the same path to self-destruction that had claimed my mother. But at least it was honest. I don't think any act I performed in honest exchange for money could make me feel as degraded as Leo did.

Except with my luck I would have gotten AIDS and died just as useless and forgotten as my mother. Or her mother—she'd died before I was born, from a botched abortion. She'd been trying not to bring another victim into the world. She was just thirty-three. When she'd died, my own mother had been seventeen and pregnant with me. My father, whoever he was, was long gone.

I reminded myself that looking back it might seem that doing skin flicks or escort service wasn't that bad compared to Leo, but my mother had made the rent on her back sometimes. She'd killed herself after a customer had brutalized her yet again. I was only sixteen when she died, and at that time I'd promised myself that I'd walk in front of a bus before I'd go to bed with anybody just for money.

Leo's cage was gilded a little better than the trap my mother had been in. She had tried to keep regular jobs, and so had I. But, like her, every time I got settled along came a man who wanted to make my life easier. I always said no. And then something bad would come of it. How could I explain it to someone like Dina? It sounded like excuses to say I had lost three waitressing jobs because the unhappy man in question had made me drop a tray of food by either bumping or fondling me, and two more because the management didn't want me saying no so forcefully, not getting it that anything short of a slap in the face was "yes" to some men. In offices, I "just didn't work out," a euphemism for the problems that happened when co-workers, some married, asked me out. It didn't matter how I answered; I was held responsible for being asked.

Poor little me, I thought. Millions of women starved and mutilated themselves to have the body I thought of as a curse. But I'd learned the hard way that while it might seem that I could open any door with my body, all of them led to someone's bed. I sometimes wondered if my preference for women came solely from my loathing for men. At least I thought I preferred women. The only time I came close to submitting to the casting couch or a casual proposition had been when women asked. More recently was the way I felt when I allowed myself to think about Dina.

Two chattering women entered, and I shook myself out of pointless picking over the past. Aside from his cruel handling of me from time to time, like tonight, Leo hadn't been abusive to anything but my soul, which, considering my future, wasn't worth that much. And my face would be on the cover of *Vogue* next month.

I could only get up because I wanted to laugh. It was funny in a way. Leo thought when I got my sixth cover I'd willingly go to bed with him. I didn't intend to live that long. Too bad I wouldn't get to see the look on his face when he realized I'd won in the end.

I joined the party, aware that my eyes sparkled with mirth. Leo gestured me to his side. He was so sure of me that it made me all the merrier.

I was flirting with a product manager from L'Oreal when the black edges of my hysteria turned to silver. My cage dissolved, and my blood sang for joy.

She was here.

Out of surprise I didn't react, but I saw Leo start, and knew he was aware of her, too. I couldn't look her way or he would notice. I knew that she was in London to go over financial matters with Leo and inspect his inventories and other assets, but I hadn't thought she would be here tonight. I remembered her light as a brilliant glow that was nearly blinding. If anything, it was brighter still. I was amazed that no one but Leo and I seemed to notice it.

Leo had arranged it, of course. He was already turning toward me.

"Look who's here, darling."

I feigned my usual mix of curiosity, wariness and boredom. "Who?"

"Ms. Financial Wizard. I wonder if she'll want to...show you her etchings."

There was no answer to be made to that, so I watched her slowly make her way to the bar and then turn to survey the room. She was looking for me, I was certain of it.

A man sidled up to her and she was pleasant in return, but he seemed to take the hint because he sidled away again. She studied her drink and raised her head to look right at me, as if she'd known all along exactly where I was.

The green in her eyes was like a warm ocean of tenderness.

"By all means," Leo whispered in my ear. "Go speak with her. But stop panting. It's unattractive."

I turned to the balcony off the crowded room, and within a few minutes she was at my side in the cool air. As she approached, the metallic scent of pollution and the harsh grating of traffic faded.

"I have to leave Thursday," she said, without preamble. "But my afternoon is open tomorrow, if you want to show me the sights. The British Museum, perhaps?"

"I have a refurbishing scheduled tomorrow," I said. "Hair, nails, dead skin, that sort of thing." She smiled as if she understood. "But I'll do my best to reschedule. There's the museum and Harrods is an experience. Like Bloomingdale's, though most Brits would slap me for saying so."

"That could be fun."

"I can't really talk for long right now." Leo would be keeping track of how much time we spent talking. Clearly, he wanted Dina and me to go to bed together, after which he would either manipulate Dina or destroy her. He had never tried to get me to sleep with anyone but him before, so his stakes had to be high. The stakes were high for me, too—I wanted to be close to her, but I didn't want to open her to his malice and spite. It seemed very important to keep him in the dark as to how much I wanted her, and how much pain, therefore, he could cause her through me.

"That's okay. I really only came so I could make a date. You weren't in when I called a couple of times."

It wasn't the first time Gerard hadn't passed on messages. I wanted to tell her not to call, not to give Leo any evidence that he was right about her feelings. But if I did, I would have to tell her the whole ugly truth about Leo and me and my very probable future.

She would try to change it. She would try to get me away from him. Her caring would give him the hold he needed to try to break her, to bend her light to his plans. I had no idea what his plans were, but they were never good for anyone but Leo.

I shouldn't see her again. I knew that. But I couldn't help myself. "Tomorrow afternoon, then. I'll call with the time and place."

She handed me a business card with her hotel number written on it. Our fingertips brushed, and I smelled fresh grasses and pine. If hope had a smell, that was what filled me.

I went back to the darkness by Leo's side and tried not to show the futility that swept over me when she left.

Dina accepted Leonard Goranson's lunch invitation with some trepidation. She hadn't heard from Christa yet as to their meeting place and time, and she didn't want to miss that call when it came. However, she did need to go over some business with him and had no excuse to avoid the timing.

She went to the address of his club, as he'd called it, and waited in an opulent outer lobby because only a member could escort her inside. She'd been killing time for twenty minutes before he breezed in, his long leather jacket spread out behind him like a black cape.

"Sorry I'm late, darling. Let's go right in."

A tuxedoed maitre d' showed them to a small booth in what was almost a corridor. She couldn't see into other booths, and there wasn't the usual clatter of a restaurant in the background. After they were seated, their knees touched. There was no room and not enough light to go over papers.

"Could we get a larger table? I'd like to take this opportunity to go over—"

"I never mix meals and business. Relax, Dina. The food is excellent here, as is the...service."

"I'm sure it is, but I do have limited time before I leave."

"After lunch, then. I promise to be good."

He's doing this on purpose, Dina thought. He knows I have plans with Christa for later.

"Here is our server now." His tone was so smug that Dina stared at him, puzzled, and then followed his gaze. Every thought of business went out of her head.

The woman wore a skintight red latex bodysuit that could have been spray-painted on for all it didn't hide. A whip was tied casually around her waist, and a chain linking her stiletto-heeled boots limited her step.

Dina stared at the so-called server, then at Goranson. She lived in New York, and very little astonished her anymore. But this was so unexpected. That a client would bring her to a club so inappropriate to business was completely unnerving.

Goranson was smiling, obviously enjoying her horror at his audacity.

Her voice unusually high, she asked, "Is this some kind of

66

joke?"

He bared his teeth. "Of course not. I thought being a woman of your persuasion you would appreciate it."

"My sexuality has nothing to do with the business we're conducting." Dina took a deep breath to conquer the angry quaver in her voice. What the hell did he know about her sexuality anyway?

"My only thought was to give you a nice lunch, my treat. If you like, she could be on the menu."

Dina gasped, so upset she could not speak. The glasses on the table jangled as she extricated herself from the booth. She snatched up her briefcase.

"Dina, darling, I was just joking. Don't you have a sense of humor?"

"When you treat women like property, no, I don't." She knew he understood she meant more than just this woman.

"But Dina, she's here of her own free will." He meant more than just this woman, too. "By the way, have you seen this yet?"

He handed her a tabloid, open to the first inside page. A full color photograph the width of three columns featured Christa and him dancing. He was dipping Christa, and her head was thrown back to reveal her lush body barely covered by the gown she had worn last night.

"Keep that copy if you want. I can get plenty where that came from."

She dropped the newspaper as if it were on fire. "Let me know when you want to talk business," she snapped.

His voice carried after her. "Christa will meet you outside the Harrods tearoom at two. Have fun."

She walked as rapidly as she could away from that place, afraid to be associated with it in any fashion. In her whole life she'd never felt like this, cheapened and insulted. It was supposed to be a business lunch. A *business* lunch.

By the time she got to Harrods, some of the anger was gone. She waited outside the tearoom until three, then had Christa paged over the next hour.

But Christa didn't come, and that little shit of an assistant informed Dina haughtily that "La Christabel was not taking calls."

Christabel leaned against the warmth of the Sacred Tree, marveling again at how green the leaves were. The sky gleamed blue above. The water from the nearby stream had never tasted so good. Sunshine had never been so dazzling. Wild mint had never seared her senses as it did every day of the most wonderful spring Christabel could ever recall.

"I'm tired, Chrissy," Bitsy whined. "Let's go home now."

The world had indeed become a miraculous place, but Bitsy Albright was unfortunately still part of it. "If you're tired, you start back and I'll catch up."

"You can't stay here alone." Bitsy sat down on an exposed root to fiddle with her boot.

"I already did, remember?" They'd only been there a half hour. Not nearly long enough.

"I still don't believe you did."

A quiet chirp from deep inside a thicket brought a flush to Christabel's face. "I did so, and if you don't believe me, ask her."

Bitsy followed the line of Christabel's pointing finger. She fell back with a gasp. "Chrissy! We have to run!"

Christabel assumed the same tone that Bitsy often used when explaining things she'd learned from her older sister. "Don't be silly. She's just a girl, like us."

"A savage. Godless. And…unclean."

Rahdonee stood watching them, her head cocked to one side. Her braided hair was slung over one shoulder and her face glowed as if she'd just scrubbed it. Christabel didn't know how Rahdonee knew, but every time she came to the Sacred Tree, as she'd learn to call it, Rahdonee would appear a short time later.

"Geraldine," Christabel said formally, "this is Miss Bithia Albright. Bitsy, please meet Geraldine Manhattan, a doctor."

"Girls aren't doctors." Bitsy still cowered on the root, her hands clutched in her dress.

"She saved my life. You know that. And she'll tell you that I slept right here that night last winter."

"It's a pleasure to meet you, Miss Albright." Rahdonee smiled politely, but there was an extra twinkle in her eye as she added, "Christabel did sleep here that night."

Christabel knew she was smiling in a silly way, but it felt marvelous to have a secret adventure that just she and Rahdonee knew about. Every few weeks they would meet at this tree and talk about anything. That was also a secret, a beautiful secret. The best secret ever and Christabel wanted her life to go on just like this forever.

Bitsy clambered to her feet, acting like a doe about to bolt. "Reverend Gorony says we should not talk to her kind."

Christabel stamped one foot. Bitsy was being such an idiot. "Reverend Gorony's been saying the sky was going to strike us all dead the last three months, and that hasn't happened, now has it?"

"Who knows when God will strike? God gives us a chance to repent. Repent and—"

"Would you like something to eat?" Rahdonee sank gracefully to the ground and opened her leather pouch. "I have fruit—" she held up a pear "—and meat."

Rahdonee was, in Christabel's estimation, one of the cleverest girls that could ever be. Within minutes Bitsy and she were chatting like old friends while Bitsy ate a wedge of pear and some smoked venison. Rahdonee even appeared to be interested in Bitsy's account of her cousin's dress, newly arrived from England.

"Two hems of lace?" Rahdonee passed a piece of pear to Christabel. "Is that rare?"

"Of course it is." Bitsy gave a patient sigh. "I wouldn't expect you to understand, but *French* lace is very dear."

"Your world is so large. Christabel tells me that the language you speak is not shared by all."

The sound of her name on Rahdonee's lips distracted her from

Bitsy's prattling reply. How could it always sound like bells? Not just any kind of bell, either. Like chimes at a temple on a hillside over a deep, still lake, those kinds of bells, sweet and strong at the same time.

She had wanted Bitsy to meet Rahdonee but now she wished Bitsy away. It didn't seem right for her to be here, under this tree, talking about nonsense when they could be listening to Rahdonee's stories about the Sky God and Great Mother, the games of the River God and the Wind God. Christabel hadn't finished telling her about Poseidon and Athena either.

The tree swayed in the light breeze and the patches of blue visible through the branches seemed to wink and tease. The whole world was alive in ways Christabel had never thought possible, and it was right there, just above her head. Just out of her reach. It was closer when she was alone with Rahdonee. She could dream anything, imagine any wonder, when they were alone.

She wasn't surprised when a hummingbird buzzed briefly near Rahdonee's shoulder. Rahdonee drew back, laughing, and a leaf drifted into her hair. Christabel wondered if Rahdonee's gleaming hair was as warm to the touch as it looked in the sunlight. When the leaf tumbled along her sleeve, Christabel traced the path with her eyes, suddenly out of breath. She would have thought herself sick except these feelings happened whenever Rahdonee was near.

"It's getting late for your long walk home," Rahdonee said. "Shall I walk with you along the way?"

"Yes," Christabel said immediately. "Let's take the path past the blackberry thickets."

To Christabel's annoyance, Bitsy linked her arm with Rahdonee's and continued babbling on about weddings. She watched the way Rahdonee walked, her feet leaving no trace on the ground next to Bitsy's heel marks, and tried to imitate the light, unobtrusive tread.

The blackberries were still tart and small, but Rahdonee seemed to have a knack for finding the sweetest. Bitsy didn't hesitate to take the offered fruits and they spent some time hunting among the brambles.

"Over here." Rahdonee beckoned. Christabel abandoned her current search and navigated her way past the thorny bushes to join Rahdonee.

"I found some," Bitsy announced. "Be there in a minute."

"This one," Rahdonee said, "is perfect." She held the dark berry between her fingers. "Would you like it, little bird?"

Giggling, Christabel opened her mouth to let Rahdonee put the berry between her lips. She closed her eyes, she had to, because the look on Rahdonee's face was no longer quite smiling and Christabel's heart was beating like the hummingbird's wings.

Nectar exploded against her tongue and the roof of her mouth and she made a little noise. "That's the best berry ever." The next words fell out of her mouth before she could stop them. "Everything is the best ever with you."

Even as she wondered how to take back such a foolish admission, Rahdonee said, "Yes, it is. I feel the same."

Simple words, but Rahdonee's expression wasn't simple at all. Christabel could hear Bitsy making her way toward them. Quick or Bitsy will see, she thought, and then she kissed Rahdonee full on the mouth.

After that there was really only one thing to do. "We're going to be late home," she called to Bitsy, and she ran for the path, her heart flying as high above her head as the trees.

For the entire rest of the day her feet never seemed to touch the ground.

Chapter 8

Dina yawned so deeply she saw stars. She blinked them wearily away as she streaked several more lines with her highlighter. The astroyellow stripes wavered. After a few minutes, she realized she'd stopped reading because it felt so good to rest her head on her hand.

Jeff sank wearily into the chair across from her and handed over a Milky Way. "Coffee has stopped working for me, so I segued to sugar."

She tore the wrapper off and took a large bite. "Thanks," she managed through her full mouth. After a swallow, she added, "Chocolate has caffeine in it."

"Who cares?" He glanced at the stack of already read pages. "I'll catch up with you. I'll be glad to see the end of this bloody project."

"Me, too. From the bottom of my heart."

"Why is this guy such a prick? He designs clothes like a god, but half of our faxes go missing—he needs to fire that assistant of his."

Since she and Jeff were alone in the office, she spoke more freely than she otherwise would have. "I think that Goranson wants to have me to blame if things don't pan out. I'm quite sure he'll insist I was incompetent."

"Asshole." Jeff's low blood sugar was showing, Dina decided, even though she heartily agreed with him.

She hadn't told him about that so-called business lunch, but even two months later it still sent a chill down her spine. Goranson wasn't sexually interested in her, but had simply taken pleasure in upsetting her. She hadn't told Jeff because it would upset him as well, and she didn't want to start any topic that might lead to her mentioning Christa. She wasn't certain she could keep her tone disinterested when Christa was the topic of the conversation. Everything Goranson was doing seemed to be about Christa, too.

"Why don't you tell George about what an idiot Goranson is being?"

"Because partners don't ask other partners to deal with the not nice people."

"But you're not a partner—oh, but you want to be." Jeff pouted at his candy bar. "I get it. No running to daddy to deal with the nasty man."

"After the deal's done, after we're all richer than we were, I'll tell him. At that point Goranson's out of my life." But I don't want Christa out of it, she could have added.

What was she thinking about Christa like that for? Two months and they'd not exchanged an e-mail or note. "La Christabel" had been unavailable when Dina had called just after the trip to London. There was nothing between them except sparks.

Jeff shrugged. "I'm sitting here thinking about what to even say. I mean, you're right, what could we tell George? The guy never argues or gets nasty, he just picks and picks at all that little stuff."

"He's trying to distract me from the larger issues, that's all. He always apologizes when I redirect his attention."

"Sure, last time he apologized to me for a fax going missing I knew he was implying I'd never sent it. It was in that smug voice of his. And who's sitting in their office at—" He glanced at his watch. "Eleven-thirty? Redoing projections again? Not him. He's at some cocktail party eating brie and caviar."

The thought of Goranson at a party with Christa, showing her off like a fancy tie clip, made Dina's heart pound. Her reaction was absurd, she told herself. Christa had the life she wanted. Overnights from Goranson always contained clippings of the latest publicity, and Christa looked anything but unwilling.

I'm too tired, she thought abruptly. I'm thinking about her again. "Jeff, go home. I can't read another page and there will be time in the morning for you to catch up. And we must spare some time tomorrow for the IOL Communications offering."

Jeff finished his Kit Kat and nodded wearily. He glanced at his watch. "And to think that I was glad there was a market upturn for IPOs last quarter and we were getting more clients. Home in time for Letterman—nearly."

Dina started to apologize for working him so hard, but he shushed her. "I'll be asleep three seconds after I get home. Oh, and take your umbrella, it's raining again."

"You mean still." It had been raining for weeks, months even. Dina had fallen victim to what psychiatrists were calling Weather Denial. She refused to believe that it could rain any more and therefore repeatedly went out without coat or umbrella. It was the end of April, for God's sake. Week-long spates of drizzle and showers and thunderstorms, broken by only a day of mixed clouds and sunshine, were unheard of this time of year. Dina chose to believe that the next day would be the beginning of spring, at last. Jeff, the picture of practicality, carried his compact umbrella every day.

Jeff lived closer to the office, and took his leave saying, "Get some sleep."

"Sure," Dina said. The last thing she was going to tell him was that some of her hollow-eyed looks were due to a recurring nightmare. It wouldn't leave her alone, that image of the hungry demon. It was just more of her mother's so-called gift, maybe. It was an image her subconscious wanted to create from the unclean feelings she got from dealing with Goranson. She'd take a pill or something tonight. No dreams.

She closed her eyes for a moment, and her thoughts turned immediately to Christa, which was useless and more than a little pathetic. She tried putting up bricks and that didn't work, so focused on the back of the driver's head, trying to be blank.

The urge formed to tell him to avoid a fare on the Lower East Side tonight—as if there was any point in warning a cabbie about that. They were always careful in that neighborhood. It was where Dina had grown up. He'd probably throw her out of his cab if she spooked him with silly warnings.

"Shut up, mom," she muttered under her breath. She wished any of these impulses made sense. She had her life figured out and turning into her mother—as much as her mother had been loved and admired—wasn't in them. She clamped her lips shut and stared out the window, thinking about old girlfriends from college and if she should call any of them to get out of her rut. After I make partner, she promised herself again. Then I'll get a life. Then I'll date someone, rent a U-Haul, get my heart broken and settle into mid-life bitterness.

Yes ma'am, that was the life she wanted.

Christa. Why couldn't she stop thinking about Christa? It wasn't the body, but it was. It wasn't the grace, but it was. It wasn't the luminous eyes, but it was. You're obsessing, she warned herself, and as bad as any stalker. The woman doesn't want what you offer, and her eyes had never said differently. They have the Internet in England, and plenty of ways to get an anonymous account. Christa could have made contact if that was what she wanted, but she hadn't. So she didn't want it. End. Of. Story.

When the cab neared the corner of Fifth Avenue and Fifty-fifth, Dina abruptly told the driver to turn on Fifty-fifth. She knew why, but wasn't willing to admit it yet. They idled in front of Leonard Goranson's building, and Dina finally got out, after asking the driver to wait. He grunted what she hoped was assent.

She'd only had to be in the building a few times in the last month, giving tours to a few favored investors who were most likely to be interested in the headquarters for the new corporation. On those occasions, however, she had always waited outside for the clients before entering. She'd never gone in the place by herself. She hoped the key wouldn't work, but it did. The alarm code unfortunately worked as well.

Something was calling her inside. She wished she could tell herself that she didn't know what it was, but she did. She knew where the call was coming from. She knew she'd been wasting a lot of energy these last few weeks shutting out the call. Tonight she was too tired to ignore it. Too tired to ignore her better judgment, either, which told her to run.

She turned on all the lights, including the floods and spots near the architect and interior-design layouts. Anything to chase the shadows away.

I'm just tired, she thought. My mind is making things up, all because mother put silly ideas in my head. None of this makes any sense. It's not real. Her reluctant footsteps echoed through the atrium as she headed for the stairs to the lower floors.

She was shivering uncontrollably by the time she opened the door to the sub-basement. The light was dim, and water still dripped. Goranson did have the lease, but the capital for renovating the building would come from the proceeds of the initial stock sale. Jason Williams was certain that this room could be made waterproof and that the source of the roots that curled through the cracked cement could be killed with a strong herbicide.

She'd only gone as far as the top step before. It took all her will to walk down the steps into the semidarkness. She was drawn to the pale and tangled roots. The room seemed filled with anguish and suffering. That anything could live in the foul air was a miracle; it was something very tenacious.

It—the calling—wanted her to do something. She inhaled with a shudder and realized the smell was right out of her nightmare of the demon. The demon's presence was all around her. And yet there was something else, whatever was calling her. It wasn't helpless, but it needed her.

All she had to do was touch it.

She didn't believe in her mother's so-called gift.

She didn't believe this was happening now.

She hesitated, her hand an inch from the smallest of the curling tendrils.

She snatched back her hand as she swayed toward it, and then scrabbled in her pocket for a tissue. Shielding her hand with the tissue, she touched the root.

Waves of warmth and tingling awareness shot up her arm.

She stepped back in surprise, and a piece of the root broke off in her hand. The remaining tangle quivered for several seconds.

She backed across the room, stumbling over the steps sooner than she expected, and bolted upward, not pausing until she stood at the alarm panel.

With shaking fingers she punched in the code, and then she got the hell out of there and into the back of the cab.

"You okay, lady?"

"Yes, fine. I don't like being in buildings on my own is all."

"Creepy. Lots of bad people on these streets."

He quickly turned toward their original destination and by the time they reached Dina's building she was feeling more in control.

That is, until she paid off the meter and found herself saying, "Don't pick up a fare at Mott and Spring."

The look she got left her in no doubt that the poor man thought she was possessed. The cab disappeared into the darkness in record time.

Her arms trembled as she dropped her briefcase and shrugged out of her suit jacket. Clutched in her left hand was the tissue and root. Her arm had stopped tingling, but a little tickle remained against her palm.

She hurried to the picture of her mother that looked most like her and stared at what was almost her own reflection. "What do I do now?" The picture didn't answer, of course, but now that she was thinking of her mother, she felt calmer. After a deep centering breath she could almost hear her mother's soothing voice, explaining what was necessary.

It felt so right, and she was so tired, that questioning was a waste of time and energy. Following the quiet instructions, she gently placed the tissue and root in front of her mother's picture, stripped out of her clothes and took a hot shower. She shampooed her long, dark hair and left it to dry by itself after a vigorous toweling. Her hair felt strange against her bare back, and she realized it had been years since she'd let it loose for more than a minute or two.

Naked, she scrubbed the top of her oak dining room table with salted water and then fetched the tissue. She turned off all the lights, turned up the heat, and opened the kitchen shades so that the white light of the moon and stars could drift over the table.

She was forgetting something. Thoughts not quite her own hurried her to the bedroom where she unhooked her mother's dreamcatcher from its place on the wall opposite the bed. She hung it from the fixture over the table and felt ready.

Sprinkling salt behind her as she went, she walked backward around the table. When the circle was closed she stood inside, a container of cornmeal in hand. Her mother had insisted a house wasn't safe without cornmeal. Now she understood that her mother hadn't been talking about electrical fires.

She took the tissue in her left hand again and sprinkled cornmeal generously over the tabletop and chair she was going to use. Then she dusted her body with it and sat down.

Great Mother, tell me of this thing.

Was that her own voice? She had no awareness of speaking, but the voice was within the circle. After several deep breaths, she carefully lifted the tissue and tumbled the piece of root into her right hand.

The images came instantly, and with a vividness that was intense to the edge of pain.

Her sisters sang stories of the Great Mother and her consort, the Sky. Above, the moon blazed with silver heat, and everywhere the orange glow of the bonfire did not reach was limed in shimmering white light. There was a flash of skirts and red hair in the lower limbs of the tree, and she smiled to herself. She had no regrets as one of her sisters disappeared into the trees with the boy she had once thought she loved. That was past. A child would come of their coupling, that she knew. The child would have green eyes.

Laughter in her ear made her turn. The lovely red hair brushed past her cheek, and she was captured again by the laughing shimmer of shining gray-brown eyes.

"You said you'd show me the dance."

They joined the circle of dancers and her entire body sang with the joy of being alive and of being in love.

They swirled and turned, chanted and sang. When the bonfire burned low, they, like everyone else, found a dry, private place in the trees. Their skin cooled in the warm night air.

"What happens now?"

"We sleep, and we will dream of our one true love." For her, there was no need to dream.

Through the heavy air came the long moan of a woman in ecstasy and the soft sighs of other lovers finding joy in life.

Rich auburn curls spilled out over the leaves. In the moonlight it seemed to glow. "I'm not a child."

Her heart beat fast and so high in her throat she could not speak for a moment. "I know."

The leaves rustled, and that exquisite face, grown more so in the last few months as she came into her grown body and beauty, blotted out the moon. This beautiful creature, not of her own people but more dear than any, put into words what she felt. "I don't think I'm supposed to feel this way. I don't need to dream."

Thundering rapture rolled over her as the kiss kindled the longing she had been unable to deny for months now. When they parted, she gathered the thick hair against her mouth. "Do you understand what you are doing? What we are doing?"

"No, but I have to do it," came the low answer. Her fingers fumbled with the ties of her gown, and she slipped it off her shoulders, and it fell to her waist.

"Great Mother." Then her fingers were touching the soft whiteness that was offered and their next kiss sealed their intertwined futures. "We will be together always, you and I. We will soul dance in each other's dreams."

No part of her held back, no joy was denied. The sweet taste of kisses, the feel of passion on her chin, the touch of those breasts to her own—

Dina snapped back to her apartment with a stifled cry. Her body ached with longing for the love she had just felt, a kind of bonding and emotion she thought was just the imagination of poets and romantics.

She sat there a while longer before rising to scuff the salt from its circle pattern and to drop the root into a glass of warm water. She set the glass on the windowsill and lowered the shades. She returned the dreamcatcher to its usual place in the bedroom.

When she turned on the lights, she blinked through a brief bout of vertigo and surveyed the mess. "What the hell am I doing?"

Rage abruptly spiraled through her, and she swept the cornmeal from the table to the floor and crushed it beneath her feet. This was all a lie—there was no magic woman with red hair. It was just wishful thinking, the result of having absolutely no social life and her overall exhaustion from work.

"Forget it, mom, nice try as usual," she grumbled to the picture. She pulled on her robe and got out the vacuum and sucked up the stupid cornmeal. "I have my own life to lead, and maybe you don't approve of how much money I make even though I give away twenty percent, or the clothes I wear, but it's my life." She stormed off the bed, only to spend another hour ranting at her mother for things her mother had never said or even implied, but that she had taken on faith because mothers were mothers. Her last thought, before slipping into sleep, was that she liked her hair up in a braid, thank you.

In the morning she wound her hair into a braid so tight it brought tears to her eyes. She pushed all thoughts of what she had felt the night before out of her mind and went to clean up the rest of the mess.

But she could not bring herself to throw the root away.

Chapter 9

"Close your eyes and listen to the tree in the wind."

Christabel did as Rahdonee asked, but she was far more interested in kisses than the wind or trees. "What am I supposed to hear?"

"The tree in the wind."

"Donee, I don't know what—" Cool fingers across her lips silenced her, but made it that much more difficult to hear anything except her heart thundering like horses against her ears.

"Listen. It's a song."

"I hear the leaves moving, the branches creaking. Like always."

"Not like always. Are the leaves moving fast or slow? Are the branches swaying or shaking?"

Christabel listened, more interested than before. She was all at once aware of the warm moist earth underneath her, the heavy scent of maple sap, and the sun that was no longer making her squint. "There's a storm coming," she announced.

"Very good. Keep your eyes closed."

She heard the buzz of a dragonfly, then a flustering beat of wings. A rustle—oh, that sound she knew. That sound she loved.

Her mouth went dry, and her body ached with want.

"You have to get home before it rains, so we don't have all afternoon as usual," Rahdonee whispered. Her lips grazed Christabel's jaw.

They had spent several afternoons together since midsummer's night, snug in a stand of bushes and low trees. Christabel knew that Rahdonee had shed her clothes and she waited, hungering, for the feel of Rahdonee's body against hers. She began to fumble with the laces of her gown, but Rahdonee stopped her.

"We don't have time to get you all laced up again." Rahdonee's fingers slipped under her chemise. "So much clothing in the way, and it's so warm out."

"You're making me into a fire," Christabel whispered.

"Keep your eyes closed."

At last, fingers against skin. Rahdonee surged into her, and Christabel filled her hands with the heavy coils of Rahdonee's hair. Keeping her eyes closed was difficult, but it made her more aware of the quickened rush of Rahdonee's breathing. She knew when Rahdonee bent her head, and she scrabbled at her skirt and petticoat, pulling them up. Delicious pleasures, more personal and intense than anything she'd ever expected. Rahdonee found parts of Christabel's body that sang for joy at being touched, stroked, and suckled. Every time they lay together, it was as if a door to great mysteries opened and each time she remained on Rahdonee's side of the door longer.

There was a moment of stillness as she caught her breath. The wind had dropped. Even the birds were quiet. It reminded her of the night she had crept out to sleep under the tree—it was as if the woods were holding their breath, too.

"Quickly," she whispered, opening her eyes. "I can't wait for you."

Rahdonee was flushed, her mouth damp. Christabel pushed Rahdonee down into the sweet-smelling grasses and kissed the slightly parted lips with tenderness, and then less of that and more of wanting. She wished there was enough time to undo her hair; she loved to stroke Rahdonee's body with it. Tomorrow, she thought, and she busied her mouth with what was needful—tasting Rahdonee's shoulders and breasts, spicy with the fresh herbs she always rubbed on her skin after bathing.

Her hand was reaching lower, to tease Rahdonee, when they both stiffened. Hoofbeats.

"One horse," Rahdonee breathed. She quietly slipped her thin deerskin dress over her head and tied her hair back with the short string of beads Christabel had given her.

The horse had stopped, but the rider didn't dismount. Probably waiting under the tree to see if it would rain. Then wind rose again, and the Sacred Tree, as Christabel had learned to think of it, snapped its branches as if it were playing a game with the Wind God. Rahdonee stealthily slipped out of their nest, and Christabel arranged her own clothes and followed, feeling very frustrated.

They skirted the trail for a while, and then the rising wail of the approaching storm made Rahdonee insist that Christabel set off for home. They parted ways after shared blackberries and more kisses. The combination was better than blackberry cordial.

She had been walking for about fifteen minutes when it started to rain, but the drops were warm and not too sharp, so she accepted the wetting as only a minor inconvenience. Ma might be upset, but would probably only make her do some extra chores. Their house was a happier place since Pa had thrown Reverend Gorony out on his ear. The memory could still make her smile. They read Bible on Sundays at home, or went to the service in Lord Berkeley's chapel, where the preacher was a lot nicer.

When she heard the hoofbeats, she shivered and knew, without a doubt, who the rider was. She had been thinking of him, and her thoughts had spat him into reality, like he'd always said about the devil. It had been that way a lot lately. She would think of him, only to find him behind her, watching. She didn't look back, but she could feel the hard anger of his approach.

He reined in as he drew aside her.

"A bad afternoon for a walk."

"The rain is not unpleasant," Christabel said mildly. She did not want to look at him.

"Still, not the best day to go so far, if you have no reason for doing so."

He knows. She told herself he could not know. He didn't know about Rahdonee any more than he knew about her escapade last winter. All he knew was that she was the daughter of a man who had humiliated him. That's all he could know. He could not see her thoughts. That was just— He just wanted people to think he could see into their souls. He couldn't.

She repeated it to herself so fervently that when he spoke again she jumped.

"Your father would not forgive me for letting you get soaked. Not after your illness this past winter."

"Quite the contrary. He knows that walking makes me stronger. I'll not catch even a cold from this."

"I cannot return to town and say that I passed you and did nothing. Come up behind." He leaned down, hand extended.

She put up her hand to wave him off, but he seized it. Before she knew it she was in his lap, across the saddle.

He held her there too long. She realized suddenly why she was always nervous in his presence. Not because he was a man of God, but because he was a man. Rahdonee looked at her with love and want; he just had want. He was as big a sinner as any man.

"Hold still," he ordered.

"I'll not stay like this," she said tersely.

"Little Christabel, I begin to think you don't trust me."

She was off balance and nothing short of shoving him back and slipping out his grasp, probably taking a bad fall in the process, was going to get her out of his arms.

He clicked to the horse, and they set off at a slow canter.

"Let me down," she said furiously.

"This is a just a Christian act of charity." He shifted her weight with arms that felt like iron bars around her. She was pressed against him, her chest against his. Her loathing grew with every stride. "You're growing up. You should be planning your wedding, not wandering alone in the woods."

"I'm not getting married," she stuttered.

"Aren't you?" His laugh rumbled through his chest, and she held her head away.

They were approaching the outskirts of the Bouwerie when he shifted her again, this time one arm moving upward so her body was fully circled and his hand hard on her ribs directly below her breast. His fingertips pressed upwards slightly, and he repeated in a whisper, "Yes, you're growing up."

She kicked the air, and his amusement was humiliating. "Very well. I offered to take you all the way home, but you know best." He let her slip from his grasp to the ground and rode off as if nothing had transpired.

She stood there for several minutes, feeling sick and unclean. Then she trudged toward home, vowing never to share another word, glance, or even a sidewalk with that swine. He was no man of God. He was no gentleman.

She wondered if she should tell Pa and decided against it. He had enough worry with the rumors of French agents gathering information as a prelude to invasion.

As usual when she passed the mill she remembered the night she had met Rahdonee. It already seemed so long ago; she had grown up so much since then. Walking back into the settlement after time in Rahdonee's world was becoming a kind of shock. The ditches in the streets stank of waste. The heat of summer lay heavy on the caked earth and dank buildings. After the delicious air of the woods, Christabel marveled that any of Rahdonee's people could stand to breathe the air of the town. Though that evil preacher called them unclean, Rahdonee never stank the way most of the men of town did, even with fancy colognes soaking their hair and clothes.

She was almost at their gate when she realized that something was wrong. A number of horses were tied up in front, and several carriages. Goody Albright was just leaving. When she saw Christabel her gaze was actually kind.

"Child, did Reverend Gorony find you? He offered to look. Your mother needs you, dear. Go in to her, quickly."

Puzzled, Christabel hurried inside, forgetting about her soaked clothes the moment she saw her mother's white, tear-streaked face.

She went to her and gasped at the ferocity with which her mother hugged her. She'd never seen Ma like this, never seen her cry in front of other people.

"What is it? Ma, tell me. What's happened?"

When it was obvious her mother couldn't answer, she looked at the sea of faces and focused on Mr. Dennison. "What's wrong? What is it?"

"There was—they were moving the cannon at the wharf to the top of the hillock. A team of six, with eight men guiding. The horses went mad of a sudden. They said it was like nothing they ever saw before—"

"Where's Pa?" Christabel shivered with dread. "Tell me."

"The horses wheeled for downhill and drug four of the men with them. The only way they could get free was to get cut loose from the horses. Your Pa managed to get on the wagon and use his sword to cut the reins, they were tangled, and before he could jump clean the wagon went over." Mr. Dennison swallowed hard, red eyed. "The horses had to be put down."

"Where is my father?"

"Chrissy, child, the wagon rolled over. He was in it."

"No."

"The cannon—"

"No!" Her mother was sobbing harder.

"Lord Berkeley will take care of your Ma, you know he will." Mr. Dennison was trying to be helpful, but Christabel wanted to scratch his eyes out.

"Thank you all for your concern," she said woodenly. "I'd like to be alone with my mother."

"Oh no, Chrissy dear," Goodwife Livingston said gently. "We want to help."

"You can help by leaving us some time to ourselves."

"But Chrissy—"

"Please!"

"All right, dear."

Christabel heard the rustle of skirts and scraping of chairs and after a few moments she was alone with her grieving mother.

She wanted to give herself over to the grief, too. But she could not take it in. Pa could not be gone. Out of her numbness another emotion took root—fear. Goody Albright had asked Reverend Gorony to find her, and he had. But he hadn't said a word about Pa. He'd even said he was giving her a ride because Pa would want it. He'd behaved improperly, all the while knowing he would get away with it because Pa would not be there to protect her.

She put out a hand, trying to ward off a future she could feel closing in on her.

I bit back a yelp as the hairdresser brushed my ear with the curling iron.

"Sorry, love."

"Hazards of the job." Other models would have had a fit, but Andy was kind to me. Besides, it *was* a hazard of the job.

In the mirror I could see Liza Brightly undergoing similar treatment. The part of me that cared enough about things like revenge—which was not all that big since I lacked the time that vindictiveness wasted—hoped Liza got both ears burned.

Liza met my gaze in the mirror. It was almost like looking into Leonard's eyes. Cruel and mocking, she encouraged her selfish behavior in the other models. Because I never stuck up for myself, she encouraged the other models to pick at me as well.

Let them pick, I thought. None of them had been, or likely ever would be, on the cover of *Vogue, Vanity Fair, Allure* or *Marie Claire.* Leonard thought *Elle* was going to be next. *Glamour* was doing a feature article about "the new voluptuousness" but no cover shot, yet, so he still owed me two covers. *Glamour's* article was more about Leonard's reengineering of what he was calling the wardrobe of a "real" woman.

Leonard's augmentation of his successful men's business and after-dinner couture to include women's social and corporate fashion had been pronounced a risky business by the British fashion press. But they rated it a good chance at success, even though he was making the disastrous decision to headquarter his women's fashion industry in the States.

I always knew when he entered a room, but I didn't look his way, not with a hot curling iron still near my ears.

"Leo, darling!" Liza blew him kisses.

Hard on his heels was Priscilla Stone, whose style column was wildly influential. "But why the United States, Leo? Won't London miss you?"

"I felt right at home in New York, and the building I've acquired is an exceptional location that I find very inspiring." He went from model to model assessing make-up and hair as he spoke.

"It's so daring, launching a brand new line of design for women as well as relocating your enterprise." Stone arched one bleached eyebrow. "I find it hard to believe it was bricks and mortar that inspired those decisions."

He paused behind me, his mocking gaze telling me that he had no intention of explaining himself to anyone. "Menswear will still be in Britain. But you've seen through my ruse, Priscilla. Christabel made me want to design for her, and why design for just one woman?"

There was more to his decision than just the logical use of an expensive bauble and I considered that his first answer to Stone might have been the truthful one. He had never talked about moving to New York until he'd returned from a trip, very excited about that building being available. It made no difference to me, I told myself. I didn't really care where I lived since I anticipated not living that much longer anyway. New York was fine because it wasn't the hellholes of Los Angeles. And because Dina lived here. It had been so hard not to send her a note at least, something, anything, but I knew that if I did I'd be doing what Leo wanted. I hadn't seen her since our arrival in the city yesterday, but I wanted to. I wouldn't turn down a date. I just wasn't that strong. I hoped she didn't suffer for my selfishness.

"You all look stunning," he announced as he crossed the room toward Liza. "The crowd is starting to filter in, and the charity people are rubbing their happy little hands together." He stroked Liza's cheek as he appraised me narrowly in her mirror. "Andy, a little more fullness around her temples."

Andy grunted and complied.

Stone was relentless. "I'm sure it's going to be stunning. And you are just too, too daring. Doing your first show in the U.S. as a charity event. A little bird told me that you're not even going to take orders tonight."

"We're really here to raise money for the children of New York, but I'll be making appointments with buyers, if they ask."

Stone drew Leonard relentlessly toward the door, but she paused in the midst of a flirtatious anecdote to exude warmth at me. "And Christabel! You are going to be the sensation of the night. What does it feel like to have every red-blooded American male at your feet?"

How could I answer a question like that? I certainly couldn't say the truth, which was that I didn't care. I fought back a blush as Andy leaned over me. "Don't move your head again," he snapped.

So I smiled with what I hoped passed for satisfaction. Stone was already distracted by the start of music in the banquet hall and she left, dragging a willing Leonard behind her.

"Thanks," I whispered to Andy.

"Just remember me when you're famous."

Into a welcome silence, Liza said smoothly, "Christa, dear, I went shopping before we left London yesterday, and I bought this darling sweater. I have to show you."

Puh-leaze, I thought. Liza cared for my fashion advice as much as I cared for staples in my eyes. I slipped out of my robe and waited in my bra and panties for the dresser to start on my hose.

She spread the salmon-hued sweater on the make-up counter.

"You know, this doesn't seem right anymore." She held it against herself. "I didn't have a chance to try it on, but I loved the color so much." She made a great show of checking the label for the size.

The lead dresser slipped the first of my shirts over my head, expertly avoiding any contact with my hair.

"Oh no," Liza moaned loudly. "It's way too big. I'll never get the chance to return it. I'm in New York to stay, no matter what. What a silly thing for me to do—I bought a ten!"

The other models burst into laughter. All of them were single digit sizes, with Liza at the smallest—a two most of the time. Liza looked at the sweater sadly, and then turned to me. "Christa, darling. I know! Maybe it's big enough for you."

A couple of the other girls stopped laughing, but most of them were smirking at Liza's deftly delivered insult. And the color would clash badly with my hair.

I could feel Andy's silent urging for me to flatten her verbally. Somewhere deep inside myself I wanted to do it. But what was the point? Liza was a creature of the same fog and darkness as Leonard. There was no proving anything to her, and no need to, not really. Long after Liza was dust, my image would live on, if only in a magazine archive.

"That's so sweet of you, Liza," I said clearly. "But I wear a twelve. Squeezing into that sweater might get me arrested for indecency."

"Or a part in a Hollywood movie," Andy added.

Liza's triumphant smirk became just a little forced. That my figure was making me famous offended her mightily. All her petty games couldn't change that the fashion industry had decided that heroin chic was bad for business. And I wasn't devastated by her remark, either. I was just no fun that way.

Just for emphasis, I gave her a full shot of *it*—shifting my shoulders as I inhaled, changing my weight to the other hip. To my surprise, she caught her breath and looked vulnerable. Then her face hardened to its usual diamond edges. The daggers in her gaze made me lean back until the dresser protested.

Liza's dresser started in on her first outfit, and the tension between us dissolved as the business of the night took over. I don't like being dressed by someone else, but my manicure and the clothes demanded it.

One by one, we filed to the wings of the staging area. Leonard's light tone with Priscilla Stone was a blind; he was extremely nervous. Many of the potential backers were there. They'd received the prospectus from Dina and knew all about the income projections and potential pitfalls of the fashion industry. What they wanted to see now was the merchandise—not just the clothes, but the driving force of the enterprise: Leonard Goranson's talent. At this level of couture, the real merchandise was personality.

He was taking a big risk, one I could almost admire. There was no usual narrow runway and blaring music. Several models who couldn't unlearn the runway strut had been left behind. The music was just nondescript saxophone jazz. The triple-wide runway was more like a minimalist stage set. The first setting was an office evidenced by an ornate oak desk and black leather executive chair.

The light was dim where we waited, but the sound of Leonard's voice carried. I hated it, but as usual I was caught in his spell.

"What I want all of you to hear today is a word you know, a word you can sing, a word that echoes not only in your past, but the past of this country. *Revolution*. It is used so often to mean extraordinary, but it really means changing old for new. Sometimes history revolves violently, and sometimes the new comes in much more gently. But when the new is radically different from the old, even the gentlest revolution can change everything."

The lights had dimmed in the audience, and the stage lights came up. I felt a thrill run through me, through all of us waiting.

"What is radically different about what you're about to see? Other designers provide elegance. Others even manage elegance that isn't painful to wear."

The music had slowly faded to nothing. Leonard was warmed

up. "My gentle revolution is about women, what women want, women with real bodies, women who want clothing that emphasizes their self-reliance, their confidence, their personal power. I propose to give women what men have enjoyed for centuries—couture that makes them feel strong, makes them feel like the women they long to be, and not the women I, or any other designer, want them to be."

I was so caught up in the irony of what Leonard was saying—since he devoted his life to changing people to suit himself—that I missed my cue. Liza prodded me viciously, and I stumbled.

By the time I passed the curtain, I was steady again. I strolled confidently to the desk, leaned over it as if to review a paper, then pivoted to stand at an imaginary window, lost in my thoughts. The other models, seven in all, did exactly the same thing until we were arranged in a semicircle.

"Skirts cut with a natural waistline." With a little frown, I shifted my weight and swept open my jacket to put my hands on my hips, revealing the fitted waist. "And shaped around the hips instead of straitjacketed." Liza took two steps forward, and then pivoted sharply back to the desk. She leaned against it casually and I knew without looking that her skirt hadn't crept up a quarter-inch in spite of its trim and form-fitting tailoring. "A woman's jacket with rib pockets so she needn't bog herself down with a purse for a short meeting." One of the other models took a small notebook out of the inside pocket, while another removed a cell phone and flipped it open. She paced while engaging in a silent conversation.

"Along with elegant utility, I offer women timeless style and with it fabrics that will endure. Natural fibers combined with small percentages of synthetics to create strength and resilience—an echo of woman herself."

I hoped my expression hadn't altered. He despised strong women. Rather, what he called a strong woman was one who had the sense to agree with him and manipulate others to his way of thinking. Liza was strong. I was weak.

I went through the motions. I hadn't realized that it would get to me. Leonard practically sounded like a feminist, but I knew he was just mouthing the words. He didn't believe them.

No one but me seemed to notice. From the brief glances I stole at the audience, I could see people on the edge of their seats, craning to see every aspect of our outfits, or just watching Leonard expound on his belief in the strength and beauty of women.

"I think women who know their own minds should get the clothing that lets them arrange the world to suit themselves," Leonard was saying. The other seven models gathered around the desk, which was not as heavy as it looked and was actually on casters, and easily pushed it to backstage. The audience laughed appreciatively.

I slipped out of my jacket and sat down in the executive chair. Then I undid the Eton collar on my thick linen shirt, giving anyone who hadn't noticed the handworked lace collar a chance to admire it. The lace had been my idea. I faked a yawn.

"And when they need a rest from arranging the world, there's no reason why even the most elegant of designs can't let them get comfortable."

I kicked off my shoes and resettled myself on one hip so I could pull both legs into the chair. Leonard picked up the shoes and pushed the chair with me feigning sleep to backstage. The audience was laughing and applauding with enthusiasm.

The curtain came down, leaving Leonard on the audience side. I scrambled out of the chair for my outfit change. Liza had already changed—she would be first out in a pretend cocktail party.

My head was caught inside the bodice of my cocktail gown when the light shifted, brightening all around me. And I knew *she* was there. I had hoped she would be—it made absolute sense that she would attend this event.

When the dress was finally settled on my shoulders I looked at her. She had been waiting for me to look. Her gaze met mine without restraint. I felt as if she was gazing at me from across a great distance, and yet she saw me clearly, with all my faults.

I was consumed with wanting to get lost in her eyes, to experience her laughter, to taste her skin. I could hardly stand up. I'd tried hard to forget, and I hadn't communicated with her and it was as if no time had passed between this moment and the last time I looked at her.

"I just thought I'd say hello," she said. "Sorry we missed each other at Harrods."

"Harrods," I echoed stupidly. Then I understood. Leonard had told her I would be at Harrods, not the British Museum. That explained that mystery, though I had suspected that was the answer. It did puzzle me; he wanted Dina and me to fall into bed but had kept us from the opportunity in London.

"I'll see you at the reception." It was a promise. I gathered up the light in her eyes and held it against my aching emptiness. It was a sensation better than any drug, and I was already addicted to it. I wanted to drown in the warmth of her, swim forever in the tenderness of her mouth.

"Done," the dresser said.

I couldn't move. There was no way I was going to walk away from her. I would have stood there like a stone if she hadn't led the way.

I was barely in time for my cue. I hesitated, breathing her in.

She whispered, "I promise that I'll see you later."

As I stepped into the stage light I heard her voice, like bells on the wind. She said my name.

"Christabel."

And for the first time in my life, it seemed like music, like prayer. Like something of value.

The gimmick of the cocktail party was the way we mingled in ever-changing groups. Dina's light made it all seem so unreal. I saw the other models clearly. They weren't just selfish bitches, not even Liza. They were doing their job, doing it well. Liza was looking at me as she hadn't really done so for a very long time.

It was like a dream, but all dreams turn to nightmares whenever Leo joins the party. We gathered around him and raised our imaginary glasses in a toast.

95

As the others wandered offstage by ones and twos, Leo linked his arm with mine. The chill of it brought a gasp to my lips.

"Remember," he whispered, with a laughing smile meant for the audience. "Let me know when she gets you into bed." He caressed my cheek, looking like the perfect suitor.

Dina had disappeared from backstage, which was just as well. I had only enough time to rush to the bathroom and throw up before I had to change into my evening gown. The makeup people were very upset when they saw my smeared face, but it was Liza's unexpected sympathy in the form of a glass of water that made me feel even more out of step with reality.

Chapter 10

Christabel sat in her misery, aware of many pairs of eyes on her while she longed for privacy. She wanted to be anywhere but listening to Reverend Gorony talk about her father.

She held her mother's hand, understanding that the comfort she received was greater than she gave. Her mother was inconsolable and terrified of the future. Their house and funds were left to her father's nearest male relative, a brother still in England, with instructions that he either provide a place for Ma to live or the funds for her support elsewhere. For Christabel there was a promise of support until she married and a hundred pounds in dowry, which made her quite eligible.

The men were already sniffing like dogs, and her father wasn't even buried yet. She knew her mother wanted her to pick out a husband so their futures would not rely on the generosity of Pa's brother. He was much older and not in good health. If he died, so could their support. To compound their uncertainty, Lord Berkeley and the majority of his household had sailed for England, unbeknownst to them, the day before her father died. He was not expected to return until well into the fall. So any support he might have provided for Ma was unknown and his aides were unwilling to speculate.

Mr. Kingston was by far the wealthiest suitor, but he was nearly fifty and half deaf. Minor considerations, her mother insisted, but she'd relented when Christabel had reminded her that she'd married Pa for love, not money.

How could she tell Ma that she wanted to be with her one love, with Rahdonee? She hadn't found a way to contact Rahdonee yet and had had no chance to slip away herself. She knew that Rahdonee could not bring back her father, but the support of her arms and the strength of her love would soothe her troubled and frightened soul.

"The hand of God is a sure hand. He can cradle us or strike us down. It is not for us to understand His wisdom, only to obey His word."

Against her will, Christabel looked up. She shuddered when Reverend Gorony's gaze engulfed her. It was as if he spoke only to her.

"And He will not tolerate the unbeliever, nor the heathen. He will cast out the impious and the wicked. He who turns his back on the Lord turns his back on life itself."

Her mother was shaking with tears, but Christabel burned with rage. He was saying that Pa deserved to die for leaving this church for Lord Berkeley's. Lord Berkeley was a Puritan of course, but he was also a nobleman. The purity of his faith was suspect, and salvation in that church uncertain at best. Reverend Gorony had been saying that all along, when he was alone with Ma, urging her to redeem her soul by returning to the true church.

"It is a sad day for our congregation. We must say good-bye to a soldier, whose valor and strength, while perhaps outstripping his wisdom, gave many among us new lives in a new land."

There was a quiet murmur of agreement and tears stung her eyes anew. Her father had been respected and loved, and she had never appreciated that until it was too late.

"He leaves behind a beloved wife and daughter, whose futures now rest in God's hands. I pledge my aid to them both, to help them find the way to God's divine forgiveness again."

Christabel twisted her handkerchief into a knot, wanting the service to be over so she could escape. She didn't want his help and was deeply afraid that she would not be able to refuse it. She didn't want to owe him anything; all that she had that could repay a debt was something she would not give him.

"We must all strive for the path of righteousness. Together we have closed two taverns, and we can do more. The demon alcohol must be defeated. We must keep our lives free from taint, and I warn you most severely. The taint of the heathens endangers us all. We must not reach for the gates of heaven only to have them barred by godless savages!"

Christabel closed her eyes, recalling the last time she had lain with Rahdonee, the sweet tenderness, the delicious pleasure. Rahdonee was not godless. She was like an angel who enfolded Christabel in wings of love. She wanted to fly away.

"They walk among us as if they were human, but they are not. They are demons themselves—and one sits among us even now!"

There was a collective gasp, and everyone began looking around them.

"She is there!" Reverend Goranson pointed to the rear pews, and people shied away from a lone figure, slowly rising to her feet.

She was properly attired in a simple dun-colored gown. Her long, brilliantly black hair was hidden under a demure cap. "I mean no disrespect—"

"You have no right here. You must go!" The preacher pointed at the door, and people nearest Rahdonee moved away to give her room to step out of the pew.

"My name is in the holy book," Rahdonee said. "I am Geraldine Manhattan. I am here to pay my respects to a generous and kind man."

Reverend Gorony pulled himself to his full height, towering over the room. Wearing his righteousness like armor, he swept from the pulpit to the thick church Bible. He went directly to the right place—he must have been ready for this moment, Christabel thought—dipped the quill in ink, then struck it through.

"Geraldine of our church no longer exists," he pronounced. "You profane the memory of this soldier by your presence."

Rahdonee's serenity was like bread to Christabel, who let it nourish her against the fear of the last few days.

"I meant no disrespect." Rahdonee looked across the room at Ma. "I am sorry for this disturbance. Your husband was a good man."

Goody Albright hissed, "Pay no attention to her, Edith, I'm sure she was nothing to him."

"Get out," several voices insisted. Rahdonee bowed her head in concession, and turned toward the door.

Horrified by Goody Albright's insinuation, Christabel gasped out, "She saved my life last winter."

"That's *her*?" Goody Albright glared at Rahdonee's back. "No better than a witch," she muttered.

"A witch," someone close by echoed.

Run, Christabel wanted to scream. The preacher was grinning like a wolf. She knew that Rahdonee had no idea of the danger if the congregation decided she was a witch. The congregation's spiritual mentor, Increase Mather, had said with scientific certainty that the evil omen in the sky was the work of witches. Pa had heard of towns in New England that drove out suspected witches by burning their farms, in the hopes of turning the evil light away.

Rahdonee paused at the threshold. Sunlight gleamed all around her as she looked back over her shoulder.

Run! She sent the warning to Rahdonee from every inch of her body, every corner of her mind.

Rahdonee's lips moved so slightly that only Christabel could tell she spoke. She breathed, "Christabel," then pushed the door open and left.

"We must purify ourselves from this evil," the preacher exulted. "God will show us the way."

Christabel sat shaking, unable to let go of the horror she had just sensed. Rahdonee, her people—they were no longer safe here, and they had no idea. She would have to warn them, somehow.

George Berkeley was a master at glad-handing. He worked the crowd in the reception room off the banquet/show hall while Dina stayed within arm's reach, grateful to let George's ebullient personality do as much to sell the investment as her extensively detailed prospectus.

They had nearly one hundred-percent commitment on the IPO, and sufficient institutional investors had signed on at the interest Dina had proposed. The public would never get a chance to buy the stock at the initial price, which was hardly uncommon. The new public corporation would run a full page ad thanking their new shareholders for their faith.

Goranson wouldn't thank anyone because he believed no one was to thank but him. Dina wished she didn't hate him. Hating him made her head hurt and she felt tired whenever she thought about him. Which, of course, would please him. She didn't want to give him the satisfaction of wasting her energy or time. But hate him she did—his manipulation of Christa was small and demeaning. How petty could he be, making sure that messages were lost and that they didn't meet for a simple day at a museum? He didn't love Christa himself, so his motives were a complete mystery.

Now they had managed to make another date, and though she'd spent the last few months telling herself she'd imagined the things she'd seen in Christa's eyes, she'd seen them again tonight. She was scared and excited and calling herself a fool and yet those inner voices kept urging her to hold nothing back with Christa and keep both eyes trained on Goranson.

"Yes, this is Dina Rowland," George was booming. "The newest partner at Berkeley and Holland."

Dina had to smile, and she let go of her preoccupation with Goranson. Her partnership had come through last week, on the heels of the Goranson prospectus being hand-delivered to the investors. George had known it would be a go. Even now Jeff probably had his feet up on Dina's old desk, likewise rewarded for his hard work.

"Tell them what my first act as a partner was," Dina urged George.

"Dina gave herself—get this—Saturday *and* Sunday off."

"And I'm going to do it this weekend, too."

She turned from the appreciative chuckles and shook hands with one of the textile representatives. She worked her way to the end of the room where Goranson, flanked by his models, was holding court. Christa was at his right hand. For a moment she was the wisp that Dina had first seen in the dim light of Goranson's building. Then she solidified. God—she was beautiful.

They were all still wearing the evening gowns from the finale. The man was a genius, Dina thought. The waist of Christa's gown came in high on her ribs, giving her a Regency air without a whalebone corset. In the finale she had demonstrated a full range of motion, too, by playing catch with another model. The bodice swept over the peaks of her shoulders, leaving her arms bare above opera-length gloves. The cameo at her throat was the only distraction from the soft column of her neck and the generous curves below that made Dina weak in the knees.

All of the models looked stunning. Their gowns were equally flattering to tummies, arms and thighs, though only Christa filled her gown so spectacularly. Dina told herself not to stare at Christa's cleavage only to find her mind preoccupied with the full curve of Christa's hips.

"And there's the woman of the hour!"

Dina jumped slightly, having been too caught up in contemplating Christa to notice Goranson's awareness of her.

She found the composure to smile even as an inner voice whispered that failing to keep track of him was a mistake. "It was a long journey to this night. I'm glad we finally made it." *And I'm so glad I don't have to work with you anymore.*

"Only because you were the harshest task master I've ever encountered. You made me behave myself."

Her right arm trembled, and she realized she wanted to bury her nails in his face. She felt positively savage, then stunned, by the rush of her rage. She tried to cover the brief vertigo that followed by gesturing at Christa. "What a lovely gown."

"For a beautiful woman," Goranson added. He kissed Christa's hand. Dina could not tell what Christa was thinking. "And speaking of which, Dina, you must let me fit you for a suit. I'll do it personally. Your figure is like...Liza's, I would say." He gestured at the model on his left. "The suit she wore would be perfect for you, in your own size, of course. You're considerably taller."

He made her height sound unnatural. Hell would freeze over before she wore any of his clothes and gave him any more opportunities to stare so indecently at her body. "And I'm a pound or two heavier."

"Don't worry," he soothed. "The design accommodates that, as long as it's fitted properly."

"Leonard, I'm really tired. I think all of the girls are. After the flight yesterday..." Christa seemed cold to Dina, as if she didn't care that Dina was there, quite the opposite of what her eyes had said in the dressing room. Then they'd shone like liquid amber. Now they were clouded.

"Of course, my darling."

"I'm not in the least tired, Leonard." Liza tucked her hand under his arm. "You know me. I can stay up all night."

"I know, dear girl, but Christa is right. You were all brilliant tonight, but tomorrow you've got to look well rested and fresh as bandboxes for the photographers. So off with you."

Liza looked daggers at Christa, who seemed oblivious to everything around her.

"Everyone," Goranson was saying. "One last show of appreciation for the women who made this evening possible. They are my inspiration."

Under the cover of the applause, he said to Dina, "Liza and the other girls will insist on at least one club before bed, so I'd be grateful if you'd see that Christa makes it safely back to the Omni. She *is* exhausted, and I don't trust the night creatures in your fair city."

Dina wanted to retort childishly, "Takes one to know one," but she only nodded. Once again Goranson seemed inordinately pleased with himself. Whatever his reasons were for keeping them apart in London he now consented to their being together. Did he understand that he couldn't play his little games anymore? Dina was sure that was *not* the reason, and she resented feeling as if she had had to get his permission to see Christa.

The models moved toward the banquet hall door. Christa said nonchalantly, "I'll be about twenty minutes getting changed."

"I'll meet you at the front door in twenty minutes then," Dina answered.

She turned back to the crowd, wanting to find George and say good night, but as she gazed over the crowd she found Goranson smirking at her. His grin widened when she was unable to hide her grimace of dislike.

He knows, she thought abruptly, and turned away, not at all sure what it was she thought he knew. She hardly knew herself.

Dina was kicking herself when she reached the front door of the hall and saw that the predicted summer storm had arrived. She had no umbrella as usual. Another suit jacket was going to get soaked.

"I don't have an umbrella either."

Dina lifted her gaze to Christa's, aware that she was not hiding her thoughts. An umbrella was simply unimportant. All that mattered was that she was here.

Christa said, in a low voice that brought heat to Dina's ears, "I don't care either."

In the formal gown Christa had been stunning, but in jeans and a thin cashmere camisole she made Dina break into a sweat. Her face was rosy and scrubbed free of the meticulous stage makeup, and her hair was down around her shoulders. She looked real, and was all the more terrifying.

"Let's try to find a cab. It shouldn't be hard." She pushed open the door and the heavy smell of wet sidewalk washed over her.

"Do you suppose there's some place open for dinner at this hour? Once again, I'm famished."

Dina glanced at her watch. Nearly midnight on a Friday. "I know a Thai place that's open. Near my apartment." She didn't know why she added that bit of information.

"That's great. I don't feel like enduring the bustle of a restaurant anyway."

Dina gulped, unprepared for the concept of being alone with Christa in her apartment. Because there was no way it would just be dinner.

There was a short queue of taxis anticipating people leaving the Fashion Center, so they were soon on their way uptown. Dina was so nervous she could hardly breathe.

"It seems like a waste of time." Christa seemed tentative. "We don't have a lot...I mean, if you have anything to munch on at your place I'd be happy with that. We don't have to get takeout."

"I have canned soup and half a baguette," Dina said. "And orange juice."

Christa whispered, "It's enough."

Dina gave the cab driver the new destination; they were almost there anyway. When they stood on the sidewalk, the aroma of roasting garlic wafted to them from the restaurant. "Are you sure you don't want to get something more substantial? I owe you a dinner, remember?"

"I'm sure. And I do remember...everything."

Dina set about making the soup the moment they were in the door, leaving Christa to wander through her tidy living room. Pedra had obviously been in during the day, and Dina was grateful the pile of dry cleaning was gone.

"Is this your mother?"

"Yes, those are all of her." She dropped the saucepan, then the can opener.

Christa was touching the collection of frames with gentle fingertips. "I remember you telling me she was beautiful. You were right."

"It wasn't just that all daughters think their mothers are

beautiful." Dina tried to control her trembling, but orange juice splattered on the counter.

"Not all daughters do, but you weren't exaggerating. I feel as if I know her. As if I could tell her anything. All my secrets."

"She had that effect on people."

"You look just like her."

"I don't think so."

"It's still true."

Dina fumbled with the can opener, having no success. Her hands were shaking too much.

Christa came to lean against the counter. Dina continued fumbling.

"I just launched a multimillion dollar IPO, and I can't open a can of soup."

Christa began to reach for the can opener, but smiled ruefully. "I ruin this manicure, and I'm a dead woman."

"So what do we do now?" Dina tried to smile lightly, but failed miserably.

Christa seemed to shiver with cold, then she whispered, "I'm sorry."

"For what?" Dina finally found the strength to look into Christa's eyes.

They were a storm, a roiling turmoil of darkness and fear. Dina wondered what it would take to bring warmth permanently into those eyes, to make Christa feel safe. "For what?" she repeated.

"For this."

Christa cupped her face and her thumbs traced the outline of Dina's lips. "And for this," she murmured, as her fingertips brushed over Dina's throat. "I can't help myself."

"Neither can I." Dina arched her neck, her body singing in response to Christa's touch. Like in the vision she'd had, she felt whole and loved for the first time in her adult life.

Christa's sob brought her back to the present. They were not young, naive lovers. Christa was trembling with fear, and yet her hands still explored Dina's shoulders and hair.

"I could never hurt you," Dina tried to assure her. She stilled

Christa's hands long enough to remove the braid clip and shake it loose. She rubbed her head against Christa's hands.

"I would never mean to hurt you," Christa answered lowly. Her fingers were unraveling Dina's braid. "And tomorrow doesn't matter. Who knows how many tomorrows we have."

As many as you want, Dina promised in her heart. As many as I can make for you. She pulled Christa to her for the first of many long, hungry kisses. When kisses were no longer enough, Christa pushed her away and walked to the living room. In the dim light she pulled her camisole over her head and held out her hands.

Dina went to her, let Christa put her hands on the lacy straps of her bra. She had already known what Christa's skin would feel like, but really touching the smooth satin brought back every aspect of the vision—how she had loved that other Christabel and been loved in return.

"Touch me everywhere," Christa breathed.

Dina promised with a kiss and where her fingers stroked, her mouth followed until their bodies stretched out on the rug, straining against each other. She trapped Christa under her and pressed her shoulders to the floor. Her languid kiss tasted deeply of promised passion.

She did not believe in the vision, and yet she knew every tender and sensitive inch of Christa's breasts, knew that gentle, persistent attentions with her teeth and tongue would release the long, crooning encouragement that filled her ears. Her fingers, equally gentle yet persistent, slipped into a welcome of soft fire.

They were almost motionless. Dina had never made love to a woman this way before. Minute attention in near silence, completely focused on the hammering of Christa's pulse. But she knew it would only be a few moments more...

A few moments more...

Christa convulsed, and Dina lost her balance for a moment. Dizziness welled up in her and she pulled the bear skin over them, drying Christabel's tears, saying it was not the last time, they would be together again, she should not be afraid.

In stereo, from within her vision and next to ear: "I can't help it. I'm so frightened."

She gasped for breath as if she'd woken from a nightmare, but lost the sensation in a new flood of feelings as Christa pressed her down and unbuttoned her shirt.

"But I have to do this. I've waited all my life to do this."

"Please." Dina seized Christa's hands and pulled them under her shirt. She arched her back and Christa struggled with the hooks. She gasped with surprise and anticipation when Christa swore and yanked her bra down. The straps bound her elbows to her sides as Christa caressed her breasts first with her cheek, then her lips, then her tongue.

Christa's urgency wasn't particularly gentle, but Dina didn't want it to be. She could feel more than her body joining with Christa. Invisible ties, like ribbons of light, were spiraling around them, fueled by passion and solidified by the gasping words that passed between them.

"Now."

"Yes."

"Kiss me."

"Be in me."

"I love you."

"I will always love you."

There was a flash of light that Dina thought her imagination until the thunderclap several seconds later rattled the windows.

They fell apart, both panting. In greater haste they grasped and pulled at their remaining clothing until they could twine bare arms and legs and start over.

Christa swept her hair over Dina's thighs. Dina had never felt something so sensuous before and yet it felt like the return of a treasured memory.

She closed her eyes.

Overhead starlight trickled through the full branches as the tree sighed in the wind.

Chapter 11

Christabel had never dreaded nightfall before, and never given much credence to the idea that evil walked abroad only when the moon rose. She believed it now. There was evil in the streets at night, lighting its way with dozens of torches.

Three nights ago the mob had burned their second tavern, and dragged the publican to the stocks while his terrified family had watched. Bitsy Albright had recounted the events with fascinated horror and her exhilaration had been deeply unsettling. Through the lifted curtain Christabel watched tonight's mob stream past their house. A gaggle of onlookers followed, mostly children and silly girls like Bitsy.

"Chrissy!" Ma's sharp call brought Christabel back to her work near the fire. "We don't have time for that. If we can get this bit of piece work done we'll not need so much charity from other folks."

She bent her head over the needle and thread, and worried about the cup Ma kept almost constantly at her side. It was only ale, true, but it seemed that Ma was not quite herself and not because of the way they'd lost Pa. "There's no more taverns left, Ma. Who do you think they're after now?"

"Troublemakers who ask too many questions." Ma nodded at the lace in Christabel's hands. "Keep the hem straight. I want to take this back to the tailor in the morning."

"What if the tailor is the one getting burned out?"

Ma gave her a sour look. "Next you'll be saying it's the pewtersmith or blacksmith. Decent folk who do honest work have nothing to fear."

Recognizing one of Reverend Gorony's favorite statements, Christabel thought it best not to answer. Every time she spoke of him the preacher would show up at the doorstep. He would always tell Ma he was there to see that they were doing well, but his eyes followed Christabel with indecent intent.

Ma's eyes began to droop and Christabel watched anxiously as her mother slipped into another ale-bidden sleep. There was a scream in the night—the mob couldn't be far. She could see nothing from the window. Not knowing what was happening became unbearable.

Pa's cape covered her hair and form well enough. The noise of a large crowd was easy to trace, and she rounded a corner not five houses from her own home to see that they'd gathered around the Dawson's cottage. Lord Berkeley had given them the summer to mend their ways and yet, it was true, waste and garbage stood deep in the street and the rats grew bold. Their house was a blight, but burning it down wasn't right.

There was an argument of some kind and Christabel made her way around the outside of the crowd. She recognized the rise and fall of Reverend Gorony's words, but wasn't sure who had the audacity to argue with him.

"This is not the Lord's work you do. The Lord gave us only two commandments. Love God. Love thy neighbor—you strike your neighbor instead."

On tiptoe Christabel could just make out one of those odd Quakers, unmistakable in the round hat. Most of their kind had gone someplace south, but she was almost certain this was the furniture maker. Pa had got their table from him, if she remembered rightly.

110

"I care for all my neighbors," Reverend Gorony shouted. "The filth of this family endangers us all!"

The mob muttered angrily in agreement. Behind the windows Christabel could see the Dawson clan gathered, waiting to see what might happen. Foolish people, she thought. If they had just done a decent day's work now and again the mob would pick on someone else. But who else? Where does it end?

"Lord Berkeley gave them leave—"

"Lord Berkeley doesn't have to walk in these streets. He has his fine carriage to keep his shoes clean."

Christabel missed her father so much. He'd not allow such disdainful talk of the man who managed to keep trade moving so families had money and soldiers could be paid, dissuading any foreigners from thoughts of attacking. Reverend Gorony wouldn't have the backbone to stand and fight an army. He'd be the first to hide behind Lord Berkeley's fine gates while men like Pa kept him safe.

"Our Lord will not forgive what you do this night." The furniture maker turned to the mob for a last appeal. "Go home. Tend to your families. Look into your hearts for God's true word. Christ came to teach us his word, directly. He will speak to you."

"You tread close to blasphemy, and for these unclean people. God has spoken to *me*. The pestilence of this family will strike us all down. It is time to do his work."

Men with torches moved forward, their faces like stone. Christabel realized Reverend Gorony had no torch of his own. He didn't need one—all of the torches were his to control.

In minutes the house was ablaze. The Dawsons were scattering into the night, carrying clothes and food, weeping and crying. She didn't know where they would go. The night air grew acrid with smoke and the stench of burning garbage. She shook her head, trying to clear her nostrils of the smell.

"You should not be out."

Reverend Gorony's voice in her ear sent a bolt of pure fear through her. She made no answer, but pulled the cloak tighter.

"The flames are cleansing. God's fire burns hot."

His voice was low and melodic, as if he read poetry. Against her will she met his gaze. His eyes glowed red with the dancing fire reflected deep, and he looked as if each scream of terror was beautiful music.

She turned, thinking to run, but he caught her arm. "Witness my power, Christabel. I can turn it to any means I choose. You have power, too."

Smoke curled down in a rising wind, making her eyes burn. She yanked on her arm, but he pulled her closer to him.

"You can stay my hand with a word. I will tell you the word very soon."

She tore herself from his grasp and ran into the night, home to Ma. Trembling, she roused her mother from her stupor and helped her to bed, then climbed into bed with her. Even there she did not feel safe.

She could smell the fire all around her. There was no longer any hope that the mob would quit. The Manhattans and her dear Rahdonee needed to be warned.

We should move to the bed, Dina wanted to say. Christa's mouth stilled any attempt at words and Dina succumbed again to the sweetness of kisses. Her earlier fancy that they were making love under a tree gave way to even more outlandish images, but none of them frightened her.

Her skin had never felt this alive—she hadn't known that it could. She was aware of *everything*, the roughness of the rug under her back, the brush of Christa's hair on her breasts, the yielding satin of Christa's thighs. She thought she could smell cornmeal and salt, and if she closed her eyes it was pine and the smoke of a lazy, warming fire. Someone was singing a song she'd never heard before, in a language she didn't know, yet it filled her with peace.

She could feel Christa moving against her, and still there was more. This time it was more than a vision, more than images she saw not with her eyes but with her heart. The hands on her body knew every inch of her and explored her with certainty.

She wasn't surprised to open her eyes and see the girl she loved, her Christabel, earnest and strong-hearted, leaning over her. The world beyond the thicket where they loved was alive and that magic was inside her now, to its fullest measure. She knew why the bee laden with nectar was lazy, why the salmon gave its life's energy to spawn. For this, for life, for the touch of these hands, she would give her life.

She laughed softly. "You are making me feel so sleepy."

"That's not what I intended, silly." Fingertips grazed between her thighs.

"I want to put this feeling into my dreams, and have it always."

"That sounds so wise." The honey-gold eyes were laughing at her. "So logical. But I'm not allowing you to sleep yet."

The Sacred Tree shifted in the breeze, and seemed to sigh in empathy for the love that flowed as deep as her roots. Christabel's mouth was sure of those places that brought tingles. She teased until there was no way to resist, and they both made those sounds of rising delight that honored the spirit animal within. And after, holding each other close with whispers and kisses, the spirit soul was honored as well. These bonds were forged without restraint and they would find each other, every turn of the Great Mother's wheel.

Dina opened her eyes as she lifted her hips to meet the force of Christa's touch. Treading in both worlds she still only had one heart, and it had always belonged to Christa. She searched those eyes for recognition, for reassurance that Christa knew this truth as well. They were glowing with desire and abandon, yes, but the shadows were still dark and real. Dina drew back from looking too closely, suddenly afraid that it would be Goranson staring back at her.

She arched to Christa's touch inside her, and knew she'd felt nothing like it before and yet it was a memory, welcome and rich. She knew it was her voice, crying out, but the echo came back to her laden with the dust of time.

We were meant to be together, Dina told herself. But something tore us apart. Someone…and she knew who it had to be.

"Not this time," she whispered.

Christa stirred in her arms. "Time for what?"

Dina rolled onto her side, coming back to the present, and marveled that she knew with certainty that a nuzzling kiss at the pulse point of Christa's neck would draw a soft, wondering sigh. She smiled into the hollow of Christa's throat, for as familiar as Christa seemed, there was new beauty in her lush, mature form. So much to learn, to explore, and their entire lives were ahead of them to do everything, including this. Loving each other as often as possible, she would bring all the light back to Christa's eyes.

Insane, I'm insane, she thought, expecting those inner voices to agree, but there was only the sound of Christa's gasping pleas. She held tight to Christa's hips, not stopping even when the coffee table tipped onto its side.

A few minutes later Christa stretched, then grinned as she touched the table. "I'm sorry. Is it broken?"

"No." Dina sat up. "I wouldn't care if it was. You can break all my furniture exactly the same way and I'll be a very happy woman."

Christa laughed and for just a moment, one simple shining moment, her eyes lit up with a glow like summer. "Careful what you wish for. You could end up sleeping on the floor for the rest of your life."

"It would be worth it, though I'd rather you were in my bed."

Christa blushed, but the warm glow was still in her eyes.

Later, Dina would wonder if that glow might have lasted had she not made the mistake of asking, "Stay the night with me?"

"I don't understand why you have to go," Dina said again. Her eyes were so wounded and I cursed myself as the cause.

I knew she didn't understand. She wanted me to go to the

bedroom with her. But I couldn't. I could be truthful with Leo, and say she had not taken me to bed. It was a silly lie, but there was a chance he would believe me. I had to go back to the hotel, now, to have any chance of fooling him.

"I don't want to go, but I have to."

"Is it an early morning appointment? What?"

Her hurt was like my own, but I had to hide mine. I'd given in to my selfish desires and now she was vulnerable. It was up to me to protect her. "Something like that."

She swallowed hard. "I want to...Can I see you again?"

"I want that, I want it very much. But we have to be careful."

She studied me for a moment, her gaze as penetrating in the darkness of the living room as in the middle of a well-lit hall. "I didn't realize. I should have. I guess I didn't think it mattered in your line of work."

Puzzled, I said, "What matters?"

"Being gay. You don't want anyone to know. I can see that, I guess. You're just starting out. Almost famous."

I hadn't even thought about the implications of coming out at this point in my career. I just never thought I'd have to deal with it. I wasn't going to be around long enough for it to matter. Of course, I hadn't counted on Dina.

I wanted to let her go ahead and think I was afraid to come out. I suppose I should have been, after all. If it kept her from Leo's notice, then letting her think that would protect her. Except it was a lie, and while I hadn't told her much of the truth, I hadn't lied to her. I didn't want to start.

"That's not the reason," I finally said.

"Then what is the reason?" She was half angry and nearly bitter with it, then all that washed out of her face. She put her arms around me. "Tell me. Tell me what it is. Let me help."

I wanted to crawl inside her and stay there forever. She offered such love and compassion that I could only whisper, as I had when she had been making love to me, "I love you."

"Then why? Tell me." Still she rocked me, her embrace gentle.

"Because of Leo."

She stiffened. "Why does he decide who you can be with?"

I let go of the secret, I even felt the pain of it leaving me, like an arrow being pulled from my heart. "I'm his wife."

The arrow pierced her; I felt her body quiver. She let go of me, not quite pushing me away.

"You could have said."

"It's not generally known."

"You could have said."

"There were reasons for it, having nothing to do with—"

"Is he safe? Are you safe?"

I didn't know what she was asking, but her anger was unmistakable.

"Just tell me. Do I need to get tested now? I know what his predilections are. And that rubs off on you. And now onto me." She turned away, her arms across her stomach.

"I don't sleep with him. I never have."

"Do you expect me to believe that?"

"It's true. And believe me, Leo thinks far too much of himself to risk catching anything. I've never asked, but I'm willing to bet he is very, very safe. Not that it matters to you." I was angry now. "I have never been with him as a wife. It was a business arrangement."

"Most people just fill out contracts."

"Ours wasn't the kind you can put on paper. He promised me something, I promised in return. I'm never going to deliver on my end. And that's all you need to know."

"And you say you love me?"

"Yes." I wanted to cry, because Leo would be so happy to know we had fought. She would never trust me now.

"It's called a divorce. And lots of people do it. It has less stigma than being gay."

She just didn't understand, and I couldn't make her. She didn't understand weakness and fear, and being born to be the victim of a vampire like Leo. If I told her that my mother hadn't been able to find a single woman in her family history that had lived past thirty-five, would she understand that I accepted my destiny? No, she would fight it and he would destroy her.

I had no fight in me. "I want to be with you again."

"When he says it's okay?"

"The longer we can go without him knowing—I just mean that it makes it easier, in the end."

"I don't want you on his terms."

"They're my terms, right now."

Dina bowed her head over her knees and I thought I saw the sparkle of a tear. "For now, then, I accept your terms," she said slowly. "You tell me when we can see each other again."

I suspected that when I told Leo we hadn't gone to bed together, he would give me another opportunity to see Dina. I didn't know how long I could play this out. All I knew was that I had to see her again, one more time, before Leo found out. I didn't even know what I was hoping would come of it. It was wrong to hope. I ought to make her hate me so she would forget about me, but I was too greedy. One more time, I thought, and then I will make her go and he won't be able to hurt her.

"I'll call you."

Dina nodded miserably. "Then I guess you'd better be going."

I dressed and relived the incredible joy of her touch. How long had it been since a woman in my family had felt as wonderful as Dina made me feel for the hour I had been in her arms?

Dina was wrapped in a chenille robe when I kissed her at the door. The cab driver had buzzed and was waiting downstairs.

She sniffed, her nose red. "Don't do this. Stay with me. You don't have to go back to him."

"If I don't, he'll come and get me."

"And you just say no to him. It's that easy."

I studied the doorknob, anything to escape from the light she was shining into me. "I can't."

"Don't let fear do this to you."

I swayed. I was within a heartbeat of putting my arms around her, of saying the future didn't matter, of saying I would stay. In the brilliance of her life, my fears seemed so irrational. What could Leo do to me that I couldn't survive? I realized then that it wasn't what he could do to me that I feared. It was what he could and would do to her.

The phone rang. I knew who it was before Dina's answering machine clicked on.

"Dina, are you there? Christa's missing. Dina?"

"I'm going to tell him to go to hell."

"Dina? I'm very worried. I hope she's with you. Please pick up. Or call me—"

"Dina, please. Just for tonight. Just for right now."

Her eyes brimmed over as she lifted the receiver. "I'm here," she said huskily. "No. No, we went for coffee. We talked until they closed. Yes, at the Omni main entrance. I don't know."

Tears were running down her cheeks. And I realized that I had made her ashamed, that I'd done part of what Leo surely wanted. I'd diminished her. I'd made her lie for me.

"She said she was still hungry. Perhaps she's in the restaurant. Is there one open at this hour? Did you check there?"

I opened the door, hating myself. Her moans of passion and happiness had long left my ears. Instead, I heard her choking back tears as she said, "Would you have her call me when she gets in, or I'll worry."

She watched me go, still talking to Leo. "She has my number." Her eyes pleaded with me. "Please have her call."

Self-pity was not a familiar companion to Dina, but she wallowed in it until the phone rang about twenty minutes later.

"I'm fine, Dina," Christa said, her tone apologetic. "I'm sorry Leo worried you for nothing."

"I love you," Dina breathed into the phone.

"I know. I need my beauty sleep. Your investment needs to be protected."

"When can I see you?"

"There's some cocktail party tomorrow night I must go to, but my schedule is open Sunday morning, like I thought. Until around two. So I'd love to see the cathedral."

"Come to my apartment. I'll be waiting," Dina whispered.

"I'll meet you there. Sorry again, Dina."

She huddled on the sofa, not wanting to go to the cold, empty bed. She didn't understand Christa's fears or dependence on Goranson. Her face would be on newsstands around the world next week and on three more magazines this fall. She was going to be an international star. Didn't she know that? What possible hold could Leonard Goranson have over her that couldn't be broken?

I'm in love with a married woman and she refuses to leave her husband, whom she doesn't even like. God, how pathetic, she thought. Her body trembled when she remembered how Christa had felt under her, and over her, and in her.

She went to the kitchen for aspirin and orange juice. In a fit of rage, she pulled up the kitchen blinds.

"Shut up!" She picked up the glass, which held the sprouted root and several leaves, and took it to the sink. She turned on the disposal and stood poised.

But she couldn't do it.

It was insane.

She turned off the disposal, put the glass on the table and sank into a chair. Very gently she touched a new, still tightly furled leaf. "What do you want from me? I don't have anything to give right now. I need right now."

The leaf shuddered, and then opened. Dina blinked. It had happened in a second or two. She felt dizzy, on the verge of hysteria. "Oh no, I'm not going to start poking my fingers so you can have the blood."

She buried her face in her hands, smelling Christa all over them. "This is impossible."

She called a cab, and then went to get dressed.

Chapter 12

The mare let Christabel saddle her, though her touch was not as expert as she was used to. She knew that there was a meeting of some kind at the church and it was her chance to slip out of the town and not worry too much about Ma being left alone.

The smoke from the furniture maker's home and workshop was heavy on the air. What was left of the structure still smoldered. Every three nights the mob was goaded to frenzied action. First the taverns, then the Dawsons, and now the Quakers were suspect. The Quakers hurt no one, were industrious and clean. If their homes could be taken from them, without any condemnation from Lord Berkeley's aides, then no one was safe.

Last night it had been the blasphemous Quaker and two nights from now likely the other Quaker family. She hoped they were packing their belongings and arranging to get off the island.

Once the Quakers were gone she knew where the preacher would turn his ire. He preached that all the Manhattans were evil, that their presence on the island was an abomination. Christabel was so ashamed that no one would stand and speak the truth to him. Instead, men trumpeted about order and the law while they broke both. Christabel hadn't understood why none of them saw how bad these events were for trade until Bitsy had said her father, and most of the wealthier merchants, had their eyes on land farther up the island.

Trying to sleep last night, with the smell of charred wood choking her throat, she had realized that from the moment the Dutch had settled the island the Manhattans were living on borrowed earth and borrowed time.

If she rightly read the fever that had taken hold inside the church, time was just about out. Rahdonee and her people had no defenses against frightened sheep that had been whipped into fury by a perpetually hungry wolf.

She set out after one last worried look behind her. Her mother was slipping away from her, further gone in drink every night. It was as if Ma was behind a shutter that closed more tightly every day, and each morning there was less of her mother there. She wouldn't have discussed it with Ma anyway—she just knew she had to stand on her own two feet. Not like a child who claimed to be brave, but like a woman who was strong.

She was her father's daughter. She could and would protect what she loved.

The gates weren't closed yet, and she rode out under her father's cloak without challenge. She flew past the Bouwerie, noticed with dread that trees were being felled to penetrate farther into the forest. She was at the Sacred Tree before it was fully dark, and she let the mare rest a moment.

She didn't precisely know where the Manhattan settlement was, but she knew the path Rahdonee always took toward her home. The moon was near full tonight, and Rahdonee had taught her not to fear shadows. She guided the mare onto the trail and gigged her to a trot.

The trail skirted marshes and groves, heading generally toward the Pole star. A wave of longing for her father brought tears to her eyes, and she trusted the surefooted mare for the next little while.

She smelled cookfires before she found any of the Manhattans. Then a lanky, tawny-skinned man stepped into the trail. He wasn't menacing, but it was plain that he wanted to know what a mounted intruder might want so long after dark.

She pushed the cloak hood back so he could see she was a lone woman. He was startled, and said something she almost understood from her lessons with Rahdonee.

"Mintoolow," she said, the Manhattan equivalent of *It's a pleasure to make your acquaintance*. It wasn't exactly *hello*, but it was about all she knew she could pronounce. With more confidence she said the only other word she was certain she could say properly. "Rahdonee."

He nodded, and she followed him a few hundred feet along the trail. They passed a sinhoteb where a woman and wide-eyed children gathered in front of the fire. The man called something to her and the woman nodded.

A few minutes later the trail widened and ended in a vast clearing dotted with perhaps twenty sinhotebs. The man called, "Rahdonee," giving it an inflection that was far more lyrical than her own pronunciation of it.

Then Rahdonee emerged from a sinhoteb on the edge of the forest. "Jiha," she said to the man, who chuckled as he said something Christabel could not follow. Rahdonee was blushing.

"Mintoolow," Christabel repeated to the man and the Manhattans nearby laughed—but it was a kind laugh and Christabel smiled, feeling a little less shy. Then she remembered her business, and swung herself from the mare's back.

A quick exchange of words and something that looked like a treat from Rahdonee's pocket, and the mare was led away by a grinning boy.

"Don't worry, he loves animals. He will rub her down and unsaddle her. He knows how."

"I have to talk to you."

"So I gathered." A passing woman said something to Rahdonee with a grin, and Rahdonee blushed again.

"What did she say?"

"Nothing."

"What?" Christabel had never seen Rahdonee look so

adorable.

"She said that seeing you she understood why I hadn't chosen any of the men here."

"Oh." Christabel felt her face stain with red. "So they know that we..."

"Yes, it's not a difficulty. But," her expression cleared, "you really should not be here."

"It's important."

They stared at each other for a long minute, not wanting nor needing words.

"And I am so sorry about your father," Rahdonee said abruptly. "I never got to tell you."

"I know—and that's partly why I'm here. I don't even know where to start."

"Come sit at my fire."

Rahdonee's fire was circled with smooth logs as if she often had company. She covered one log with a soft deerskin before letting Christabel sit down. She then offered a wooden cup of steaming broth she poured from a heavy kettle that sat just at the fire's edge.

An older, heavyset man walked up then, and, after giving Christabel a nod of greeting, spoke to Rahdonee.

"This is Sinhaya. He is our leader, and he wishes to meet you."

Christabel rose, curtsied, then said, "Mintoolow." It was a very useful word, as it turned out.

He inclined his head and replied in kind, then offered a hand so Christabel could gracefully retake her seat. He spoke to Rahdonee again and turned to go.

"Rahdonee, he should stay. I have to warn you. All of you."

He turned back at her words and settled on the log across the fire from her. Christabel was glad of his presence. She needed to focus on what she had to tell Rahdonee and not get lost in wanting Rahdonee to hold her and kiss away her fears.

"I think that some of the Puritans are going to try to drive you off the island. He's been—the preacher, you remember him?"

"I'll not forget him, ever."

"Well, he's been telling lots of people that you're evil. And some of them want to believe it. They're afraid of the omen." She pointed at the streak of light, closer now than last winter.

"That is the Sky God's eye upon us," Rahdonee said. "He looks down at the Great Mother sometimes. There are none alive who saw it when last he looked, so we are blessed."

"I like that explanation," Christabel said. "Pa thought it was just a different kind of star. But some of the people are scared that it means the devil is at work. And he, Reverend Gorony, makes them more afraid. He tells them that what happened to my father was an act of God. Punishment because he defied the true word. And he says you're all evil. And if we're to be saved, you have to go."

Rahdonee looked genuinely perplexed. She spoke to Sinhaya. His final words, after a lengthy exchange, made Rahdonee's chin quiver.

"Sinhaya says that the elders have expected this, but not quite so soon. A place is already chosen, and we will begin the move in the morning. He had hoped we could take the harvest with us."

"It's the weather," Christabel said. "The ground is more solid. They can move faster. And Lord Berkeley is not here. But I'm not sure he would stop them—it's as if his rule doesn't exist. It's all been handed over to that preacher."

"He has a dark power," Rahdonee admitted. "And such power grows stronger before it wanes."

"They have muskets, some of them. They've been burning people out of their homes."

"I know," Rahdonee said. "We are not warriors. The Dutch settlers nearly killed all of us before letting us settle here. Our tribe is only now beginning to grow again. We wish to survive. Our boats are all repaired. We even made two more. Sinhaya says that the Oneida had warned him that your people have a great hunger for land."

Sinhaya said something as he left them. He called out as he walked to the largest of the sinhotebs. Men left their families and fires and one by one followed Sinhaya inside.

"They will act quickly. You don't have to fear for us."

"I fear for you," Christabel said quietly.

"I'm not going."

"You have to. I don't think the preacher cares about the rest of your people. He wants you gone. And if he whips up witch fever, they could...hurt you. And it would be because of me."

"What are you saying?" Rahdonee took Christabel's hand and looked directly into her eyes.

She shakily related the preacher's behavior to her from the moment her father had died, and since. "I won't let him have me, but to keep him away, I have to...marry someone."

"I do not understand your people. To be safe you must be the property of a man?"

"Not property, but protected by, yes."

"You can come with us. My people will make you welcome."

Christabel closed her eyes, savoring the press of Rahdonee's fingers against her palm. "I want to say yes. I would say yes, except I can't leave my mother. Not now. Maybe when we know for sure who'll take care of her and where she'll live. She's defenseless. But until that's settled, he'll be after me. He'll be after her. Every time he talks to her, she gets more frightened. She'll do almost anything he says. I know it's a matter of time until she starts urging me to marry him, for my own sake." Her throat ached as if she'd swallowed a stone. "I don't know her anymore, but I must stay."

"It was selfish of me to ask." Rahdonee drew a deep breath, and Christabel realized her serenity was badly shaken. "You cannot leave her in his power. But do not say yes to him, because I will wait for you. I will visit you and tell you where we have gone."

Christabel nodded numbly, certain she would never see Rahdonee again.

"Your mother will expect you soon."

She shook her head. "She thinks I'm at the Albrights."

Rahdonee smiled wanly. "The old excuse again? Were you planning to sleep under the tree tonight?"

125

Christabel sent an answer through her own fingertips, which brushed the back of Rahdonee's hand. "I know who my true love is. I want to spend the night with you."

Rahdonee's brilliant smile brought the first warmth to Christabel's heart in nearly a week. "Go inside," she said, "And be comfortable. I have to take care of the fire."

In the privacy of the sinhoteb, Christabel removed all her clothes, wanting this night to have nothing held back. Rahdonee slipped through the opening and tied the flap shut.

"We can be alone," she murmured, "because I am the medicine keeper, and right now there is no one in my care."

Rahdonee discovered the tears on her cheeks and whispered, "Don't cry. There is always hope."

Christabel let Rahdonee pull her down. "I'm frightened. I can't help it."

Rahdonee pulled the bearskin over them, and then dried Christabel's tears. "Don't be afraid. This won't be the last time." Her gentle touch was a promise. "We will have forever," she breathed.

"I did not go to bed with her! I told you."

"You're lying. You smell like sex."

"I smell like steak and grilled mushrooms," I snapped. My stomach rumbled to make a liar of me, but he didn't hear.

It was clear he didn't know what to believe. "If you didn't sleep with her, why ever not?"

"She didn't ask." A very true lie.

"But when she does, you're going to say yes."

"Maybe," I said. "Maybe not."

I didn't expect the slap. Leo checked himself just before the blow landed, and it wasn't very painful, but it scared the shit out of me. He'd never directly struck me before.

"Listen to me, darling," he said fiercely. "You will get her into bed, and then you'll tell me it's done. I made you and I can take it all away."

"You have something to lose, too, if you throw me back in the gutter."

"You may be one of a kind, but don't fool yourself into thinking you can't be replaced." He grabbed me by my hair. "This is something you must do, and you must tell me when it's done."

The door to his bedroom opened. "Leonard, darling, what's going on?" Liza peered out with feigned sleep, but her eyes were bright with curiosity, and it was plain she expected a show of jealousy from me.

Leo let go of me. "Now go to bed. And no matter what, the next time you see her I don't want you to come back until she's fucked you."

"Fucking people is what you do, Leo."

He twitched as if he would slap me again, then he slowly smiled. It made my skin crawl. It was as if my defiance pleased him, as if I had become a bigger fly for him to gleefully crush. Instead of a slap, he stroked my cheek. "And don't you forget it, my love."

I turned my back on him and Liza's naked silhouette. I knew my resistance had spared Dina something already, but I didn't know what. I couldn't even guess.

I knew Leo had no desire to get mixed up with the police, so I couldn't fathom what he was planning for Dina. But it was not going to be pretty, and I had spared her a day or two until it happened. And maybe I could find out what it was and warn her. I owed her that at any price to myself.

I stood in the darkness of my room and remembered her saying "I love you." For that moment of happiness I owed her more than I could ever repay. If there was anything I could do to spare her from Leo's evil spite, I would do it.

And then, as if a thick curtain pulled across the last light I would ever see, I knew the dark truth. This what was what Leo had wanted all along, for me to have a reason to be willing to do anything he wanted.

Chapter 13

The Great Mother was calling her. Rahdonee stirred, felt the soothing warmth of Christabel next to her and wondered what it was that needed her attention.

The brush of many feet through the clearing outside was unusual so early, but they moved with quiet, unhurried purpose. The first boat was being readied in the first light of day. Sinhaya's eldest would secure their new settlement. It was a day's walk from the nearest town, and she could only hope it was far enough.

The Great Mother stirred in her mind again and she dozed, seeing the first boat leave, then the others with Sinhaya's other boys. Her dream became drenched with rain, the tears of the Sky God, and the boats scattered in the rising gale of the European hunger for land.

Christabel's hand drifted over her stomach, then patted her gently. "It's okay, sweetheart," she murmured.

She had never before hoped for the Great Mother to be wrong, but she hoped for it now. How could the world be so small that there was no place her people could rest? We all feed on death, the Great Mother reminded her. But we honor the deer, the bear, Rahdonee answered. These white men dishonor what they feed on, and make us no more than animals so their feeding is not just all right, it's necessary. It's what they call *moral*. I do not understand them.

You read their holy book, the Great Mother reminded her. Even they know that Evil finds its excuse in the words of Good.

Almost fully awake now, Rahdonee could picture the preacher in her mind's eye. Evil walking as Good—his thirst was not for land. He wanted something more precious.

"Ssh," Christabel soothed. "Sleep a little more."

There was no hope of that, but Rahdonee drew Christabel close. The preacher was not a god, but he acted as if all he saw was his to consume. She would come back for Christabel and her mother, and he would not have this one thing that he wanted. She could not save her people's way of life, but Christabel she could and would protect.

After a last pleasant dalliance, Rahdonee slipped outside for water and returned to convince her sleepy love to wake up and dress. She shook the shadows from her mind and kissed Christabel's eyes. They finally fluttered open and stayed that way.

"Time for you to go, my love."

The dazzling honey brown threatened to draw Rahdonee in for another pleasant hour under the skins.

"No, you must leave now."

"I had the most beautiful dream," Christabel whispered. "That you and I were never apart. That we were free to be together, always. And that there were oranges all around the year—isn't that funny?"

"Very funny, and you must go. I have a lot of work to do today."

Christabel sighed, and then went about making her toilet. When they emerged into the cool early morning air, cheerfully teasing *Mintoolows* were called to Christabel.

Rahdonee drew out a handful of herb nuts for the boy who proudly brought the properly saddled mare to Christabel, but

Christabel stayed her hand. From her own pocket she drew an English coin. "I don't know if he'll have a chance to spend it, but it's nice to look at, too."

The boy was pleased enough, running off to show his friends. Rahdonee walked with Christabel to the path that would take her back to the town. Once they had some privacy in the trees, she gave Christabel a gentle kiss.

"I promise I will see you again."

Christabel's kiss was more fervent. "I will wait, for always, I promise, too."

Still, her heart ached as she helped Christabel up into the saddle, because she knew it would be a long time before she was held in the loving gaze of those fascinating brown eyes. A shadow passed between her and Christabel, and she wondered at it. With a mental shrug, she decided it was her restless dreams catching up with her. But if harm was to come to Christabel, surely she would know. The Great Mother had set her to watch over Christabel and would have sent warning if she was not to let Christabel go home to her mother, who needed her.

Comforted by that, she let her worry for her people take over, and she spent the day harvesting the herbs that were ready or nearly so. They would have need of seeds and medicines in their new home.

As she had on her journey up the island, Christabel stopped at the Sacred Tree to let the mare rest. She knew she had to hurry if she was to enter the gates with the usual press of early morning vendors, thereby possibly escaping notice under the cover of her father's cloak. She patted the mare's neck as she had seen her father do a thousand times. Yesterday she had been despairing of losing Rahdonee forever, but today her heart was light.

She gigged the mare onto the trail, but something black snapped under the mare's nose, making her rear and lash out with her hooves. There was a raw curse as the mare came down and lunged forward with her battle training. Christabel lost her seat, and the mare bolted.

She couldn't breathe for the few moments she might have used for escape, but by the time she could, he was already on her.

"You shame your father's memory. Which of the savages is your lover?"

She twisted, but his strength was far beyond hers. She would not escape through brute force.

"I'll not answer to you. You are *not* my father." She glared into the preacher's sneering face.

With an assurance that shook Christabel's confidence, he said, "I'll soon be your husband. But not until I'm sure you don't carry a savage's child."

"I've lain with no man," she shot back, understanding now what she hadn't understood last winter, about how Eliza Albright had had a baby without a husband.

His gaze bored into hers until she wanted to scream from the intrusion. His glare became almost a smile. He gazed down at her body; her lacings had come untied in their struggle. "Then it's the demon witch herself." He buried his lips against her bare throat and she felt the hideous wetness of his tongue. "I shall enjoy driving her presence out of your body."

"I would rather die first." She meant it.

He laughed, seeming genuinely amused. "No, you'll ask me to do it. You'll beg."

He helped her up and merely pushed her aside when she tried to strike him. When he turned his back, she couldn't help herself, she leaped on him, clawing at his ears, his cheeks.

He cursed again and spun around so she lost her grip. He grabbed her by her hair, delivered a single blow to the side of her head, and left her sobbing on the path.

"Remember this," he said, before he left, "You are my property, even now. You will beg to be my property."

Never, she thought. Never.

When the mare came back a few minutes later, snuffling with concern, Christabel longed, with a truly physical ache, to go back to Rahdonee and run away. But that meant leaving her mother helpless, and that she just couldn't do.

The cab driver didn't even give Dina a funny look when she got out on deserted Fifty-fifth Street in front of a dark building. She told him not to wait and he gladly sped off into the night.

"Madness," she muttered. Exhausted didn't even begin to describe her physical state. She was spent from the stress of finishing the Goranson IPO. Seeing the high stakes pay off for the client and investors alike was an incredible high. She'd received her partnership, too, and the new stress of the position was already taking its toll. She was equally distressed because she had made a man like Goranson wealthy and hadn't told investors what kind of creep she suspected he was.

But what did she know? That he was probably a sadist in the bedroom? That was a big so-what. She had acquaintances who practiced S/M and made no secret of it. They were nice people, too. But Goranson took sadistic pleasure in almost everything he did, just because he could. How was she supposed to put that in a prospectus? She hadn't even been able to convince George Berkeley, and George trusted her.

Her fingers trembled as she punched in the alarm code. Who was she kidding? The business matters were stressful, yes, but she wasn't here because of business.

Christabel—she was here because she loved Christa, because holding her, kissing her had liberated something inside Dina. Whatever that something was, it had become a steady, driving pulse when Christa had walked away. The pulse whispered, "Not again, not again." It drew her here, and here she would get answers. Possibly more answers than she could handle.

"You were right, mom," she muttered as she made her way to the sub-basement. "I ought to be really pissed off that you were right, but that would only work if I had a clue what you were right about. What is it I don't know?"

Her voice echoed in the empty rooms, but she felt better for thinking about her mother. If she was indeed losing her mind, there were definitely worse things to have in her head, while she went bonker kitties than her mother's implacable, immutable, quiet strength.

Goranson got his cash Tuesday morning and Jason Williams would get his bond to start work the same day. But for now, the tangled roots in the sub-basement were still curling through the wall. If anything, they were thicker than before.

It was not her imagination that they quivered when she turned on the light. She wondered why she wasn't afraid now, then realized she had no control over her feet. They calmly took her down the steps, across the room.

Just as calmly, her body sat down next to the roots, using her light jacket to buffer some of the cold from the concrete. She watched herself get more comfortable, and from far away, she saw herself reach into the coil of roots and grasp them firmly.

A rhythmic beeping shook her from the sight of her still body. She blinked, and her mother was smiling gently at her.

"I have to tell you something before I go," her mother said.

Dina did not want to be here, but she looked around and there was no sign of her body.

"You didn't pay attention the first time, so I will tell you again."

This was not her mother.

"We are all your mother. Lie on the bed with me. Let me hold you close."

All at once she remembered the demon's presence in her nightmares. It was close now, as if it lived in this room.

"As long as you are in my grasp, he cannot hurt you. But he grows stronger and we have little time."

The heart monitor beeped a little faster as Dina nestled on the bed. She had no awareness of her body, or of her mother's, but she was not floating. She was afraid, but then, through the acrid scent of hospital disinfectant, she smelled the faint sandalwood of her mother's hair.

The simple happiness of childhood washed over her, and she knew she was safe.

"Listen carefully, this time. There is no need to grieve. I am gone. You know that. So listen."

She listened to words she'd heard before. It was not so much her mother telling her again as it was her remembering much more clearly.

"You know that your heritage is a mixed one, and that it includes the blood of the first people, who only had a name for themselves after the second coming of the white men. But when the first white men found them they were few. Some stayed, some took wives, and you are their daughter. And the Great Mother blessed their daughters with gifts."

I don't believe any of this. Dina tried to stop remembering her mother's warnings. But the words came anyway.

"For uncountable years there were several green-eyed children at any time in the lives of the first people. After they were driven from their home on this island, there was only one. And so it has been for these many hundreds of years as the people scattered to the winds and lost their name. Only one Green at a time. I was Green. When I am gone, you will be Green."

She wanted to say this was superstitious nonsense, but her mother shushed her gently.

"You already know this. You already feel the guiding hand of the Great Mother. You see others in need and you speak to it. You reassure, you help."

"No, mother, I don't. That's you. I'm not that good."

"Child, you must listen. There is a debt and unfinished business. You must look to make the debt right, to finish what was left undone."

"What is it? What am I supposed to do?"

"You will know when the time comes. I do not know what it is or I would tell you. What I know is that in my lifetime I was not called. I searched but did not find it."

This wasn't fair. Some voice from the past wanted to lay some sort of burden on her, and she already had all she could handle right now. She had come for answers, not more questions. "What about Christabel?"

Her mother's gaze unfocused, then she said slowly, "That name is the sound of bells to me, but I don't know why. You should listen, though. I do know that she is part of this."

"She doesn't want my help."

The gentle visage started to fade as an understanding smile curved her mother's mouth. "What does that have to do with it?"

"She's a grown woman. She's made up her mind and who am I to try to change it?"

"You are Green. The one who will know what to do. Listen to your soul. Do you understand?"

"Yes. No."

There was the tender stroke of her mother's hand on her forehead, then the shock of cold stiffness in all of her joints.

She turned her head and studied the roots that had gently, almost lovingly, enclosed her hand. She was no longer afraid. Not really.

But you should be. Evil is strong.

She was out of her body again, this time looking at a clearing with deserted campfires and poles stuck in the ground, but no skins wrapped around them to make them homes. In the last glow of sunset they looked like abandoned stilts of the ancient gods Christabel had told her about. There were no people, and her eyes filled with tears.

She had turned to the river that would take her to the last waiting boat when the earth spat up the demon. He blocked her way and she screamed to the others to leave her.

She fought with the demon. She was not a half-woman, strangled by corsets and convention. She would defend herself to the death. She kept getting up when he knocked her down, using her teeth to escape him, her knowledge of his sensitive places to wound. The struggle took her beyond the trees, and she could see the boat only a few feet from shore, still hoping she would come.

She broke free and ran to the water. The river mud sucked at her feet, but she was going to make it. Sinhaya himself reached for her. The air split with the crack of musket fire, and Sinhaya fell back, his chest bleeding in several places.

The demon would kill them all, she realized. She pushed the boat out into the river, shouting for them to save themselves, and then turned to face the preacher, for he had come for her.

It was not his musket that aimed at her heart, but one of his victim's. She caught the man's wild gaze for a moment. *Great Mother, I gave him aid when he asked it of me. Surely he will not—*

When the blast came, she let the force of it push her back into the water, and she floated on the river, trying to assess how badly she was hurt and if she could guide her passage without the demon suspecting she was still alive. She prayed that the boat was safely gone.

Her vision wavered, and her head went under long enough that some water was forced into her lungs. She no longer cared if he thought she was dead, but she found that her arms wouldn't pull her up. She was going to be swallowed by the river.

She turned her thoughts to the only thing that mattered now. *Christabel.*

Dina finally stirred. She was cold all the way through, and her butt had gone to sleep. She ran her hands over her skin, touched her face. She was alive, and not soaking wet. Alive, but completely empty, as if she had lived days in minutes.

There was more to know, but she extricated herself from the hold of the roots. Before she could do anything else, she needed to rest and to eat.

She knew what the debt was now, and the unfinished business. She had recognized the face of the demon.

There is more.

Dina's vision blurred as she steadied herself. Food, energy—she had to have some or she wouldn't be ready. The roots quivered and she resisted the call this time.

She didn't need to understand anything about the past except how it affected the present. Right now she knew what she had to do: get Christa away from Leonard Goranson, even if she had to kidnap her to do it.

"They're gone, and we're saved!" Bitsy was radiant with the news.

Christabel's heart sank at the thought of that quiet community no longer nestled in the woods. She examined the nearest market stall to hide her expression. "All gone?"

"Every last one of them. Reverend Gorony says the light in the sky will leave us now."

"I've got to get something for supper." The change of subject was fruitful, since Bitsy liked to show off knowing where the best bargains were. Ma wouldn't eat much, but Christabel tried to get something down her at night before she gave into the numbing of the alcohol. Even the very valuable liquors Lord Berkeley had given her father—all the way from France, he had said—were nearly gone. Ma drank and drank. Pa would have understood right away if Christabel had told him she thought the preacher was evil. He'd have probably chopped something off the preacher if she'd told him he had touched her. She missed Pa, but she wasn't sure that even he could save them from the kind of spell the preacher was weaving. It was as if the gods sported with them, as in the Greek tales, to find out what and who had power.

"The turkey's fresh here." Bitsy paused at a stall. "My ma said that I was to ask after your ma."

"She's still very sad," Christabel said honestly. She wasn't about to tell Bitsy that her mother wasn't capable of comprehending what was happening in the town, nor what Christabel told her about the preacher's behavior.

When Christabel had tried to tell her, Ma had barely surfaced from the depths of despair, saying, "He's trying to save you from the devil. The devil took your father for my weakness. I forced him to bring that witch here."

"She saved my life," Christabel had answered. "He's the one trying to take payment for it."

137

Her mother hadn't answered. Every hour she seemed to go farther and farther away.

Bitsy asked for a dressed duck while Christa contented herself with a packet of venison. She was aware of the cross look the butcher gave her and knew their bill was mounting. There was no means to pay him.

Bitsy finished haggling over the price of her duck and they walked together toward the market entrance. "You'll let her know my ma was asking?"

"Of course." Christabel wasn't certain her mother would remember if she did, but she would pass on Goody Albright's polite attentions. "Oh—what are they nailing up?"

Bitsy stood on tiptoe to peer at the long parchment that had just been hammered to the market entrance. "Says that all abandoned buildings and the land they're on revert to the ownership of Lord Berkeley."

"Like those Quaker properties?"

"Ssh. There's more. The cost of clearing the land is to be borne by the owner who abandoned it."

"That means none of them will come back to claim it." Christabel stared at the notice, aghast at the wicked partnership in play. Sinhaya was right—the appetite for land was enormous. To take it, men only needed a leader who would stop at nothing. The omen in the sky was a warning from Rahdonee's Sky God about these times of peril, but the evil was the preacher himself.

She came home from the market with the meager supper, her head full of worries. She set the latch to the door behind her and noticed that her mother hadn't even opened the shutters. Her eyes adjusted to the darkness and she realized they were not alone.

His gaze was mocking and indecent. "They were not all gone when we got there last eve," he said, without preamble.

It was a moment before she understood him.

Calmly, he filled her mother's cup from a flask of his own. "We chased some of them into the river."

He wanted her to ask. But she could not make herself do it.

She set down her basket. "How can you give my mother alcohol? Demon alcohol, you call it."

"I am doing God's work," he said silkily. "Can you say otherwise?"

"I'd scream it from the steps of the church if I thought anyone would listen." In the basket was the knife she'd used to cut her hard cheese. Her fingers closed on it.

"My God-given power is beyond your comprehension. I am the instrument of his taking this new land to his bosom. The unbelievers shall not have this virgin land. It shall be the land of the strong."

She kept her grip on the knife, not liking his gaze on her body. "I've brought dinner," she said to her mother.

Her mother drank from the cup and said nothing.

"You will be a beautiful bride, and on our wedding night you will know the power of God."

"I told you I'd die first."

"Your mother has consented to the marriage."

She stared at her mother's nearly unconscious form. "I'll die before I'll let you bed me."

"Do you remember what I said?"

"The devil has truly rotted your mind."

His expression made her shiver. He crossed the room in two slow steps. She gripped the knife, wondering if she dared use it. If he touched her, she would.

"You are more beautiful than the first day I remember looking at you."

"You aren't supposed to notice women. Aren't we all the daughters of Eve, tempting you to evil?"

His voice was low, and he spoke so intently she found herself listening in spite of herself. "But, as you've pointed out, I have no need to fear evil or the devil himself."

He seized her so suddenly that the basket clattered to the floor, and the knife with it. He looked at the knife and grinned. Holding her firmly, he stooped to pick it up.

He brought the point to her throat. "We will have an

interesting marriage. But you won't harm me. Look at me."

She did, and it was her undoing. She felt the invasion of the feral red gleam and was helpless. Gazing into her eyes the whole while, he cut the ties on her gown and then the knife went through her underclothes to prick her stomach.

She was panting with terror, willing herself to blink, to faint, to somehow break the spell of his eyes.

"She touched you softly, didn't she? She was gentle and sweet, wasn't she?" His hands were inside her gown. "I shall make you forget that there is such a thing as a gentle touch." He pinched the soft flesh on her ribs, then cupped one breast so tightly that tears came to her eyes.

Please God, help me. She remembered that his God was no friend of hers and she prayed instead to Rahdonee's great spirit. Great Mother. Deliver me, by any means.

From the corners of her eyes she saw a shadow rise up behind him. Their largest cast-iron pan struck him on his shoulder.

She was freed from his gaze and her helplessness. She shoved him away with all her rage and cast about frantically for a weapon.

Her mother spat at the preacher, then slurred, "You are no man of God. My husband was right. You'll not have my daughter!" She raised the frying pan.

Christabel gripped the fire iron. "Get out or I swear I'll kill you."

Unbelievably, the preacher laughed. She was suddenly aware of foul air, a stench like a blacksmith's forge. "Mother and daughter lionesses. I told you we chased them into the river, didn't I?"

Christabel raised the fire iron higher, dreading anything he would say.

"We pulled one very beautiful savage out of the river. Wounded, but she'll live. As long as I keep her alive." His hand went in his pocket and he drew out the strand of beads she had given Rahdonee. She had last seen them tying back Rahdonee's hair. "Do you remember that I said you'd beg?"

"No!" She lunged at him with the fire iron, catching him on

his neck. But he sidestepped and tripped her, and kicked her as she fell.

She could not breathe in. She raised herself from the floor, only to lose her balance. Pain radiated in her side and back. When finally her lungs sucked in air, the pain made her see gray, dancing rags. Her mother cried out as Christabel fell into darkness.

Chapter 14

I was startled when Liza sought me out. We'd all spent an exhausting morning being photographed for *Women's Wear Daily*. Liza had probably had less sleep than I, but had managed, as I had, to make it through the session with the flawless grace required of us.

She closed my bedroom door behind her, looking uncertain and wary. "I have to know." She stopped, then seemed to cast about for words. "I thought you married him just to get ahead. I didn't want to admit that...that you'd be a star without him. I didn't really see it until last night."

She crossed the room toward me, clad in a bathrobe similar to mine. The scent of the same skin treatment I was wiping off clung to her. She perched on the edge of my bed, and we studied each other in the mirror.

"You are beautiful," she finally said.

"Liza, I don't need—"

"Let me finish. You don't need him. But I do. After I heard you last night I realized he's hanging onto you, not the other way around. So I don't understand why you don't leave him."

Mostly curious and certainly not jealous, I asked, "So you can have him all to yourself?"

"Like I said, I need him. Sure I'm a size two and I'm striking to look at. But there are a lot of women who look just like me, or near enough. I need him, or my career ends with the first wrinkle."

"I can't leave him." As the fame started to mount, as the immortality I had craved for myself and my mother, for all of us, became more certain I might have realized I could leave him. But now there was Dina, and he had brought Dina and me together in perfect calculation to strengthen his hold on me. I knew he would hurt Dina to control me, and I couldn't think of a way out. There was no restraining order or threat that a man like Leo would obey.

I expected anger or incomprehension, but Liza only pursed her lips. "I know you think he's the ticket to the top. But as famous as he's going to be, he's not like a movie director or a producer. And you could have any of them with a flutter of your eyelashes."

"I don't…" I was the one searching for words now. "You know that Leo and I don't—"

"Yes, he told me. He's saving you for some big moment. He's so superstitious."

That had never occurred to me. Leo, superstitious? "I don't want to, not with him, not with any man."

Her lips parted and the hardness of her usual expression cracked. She stood abruptly, and then gently put her hands on my shoulders. Her lips brushed the tip of my ear. "God, Christa, do you think you're the only one?"

I let myself drink in the sweetness of another woman's desire, just for a moment. After all the cruel bitchiness, the moment was healing. She turned my head and kissed me. It was almost chaste.

She regarded me in the mirror again. "I've wanted to do that for a long time. I didn't know how much until last night. You looked like someone had lit a spotlight inside of you."

Dina had done that and I was the instrument of Leo's malice toward her. "Liza, if you feel this way, how can you be with

143

him?"

"That's just business." Her expression was hardening again, and a bitter twist ruined the beauty of her lips. "I've been trying to fuck my way to the top all my life. I have what men want, but they don't get it until I get what I want. Leo's as high as I'm going to go. You could go anywhere."

"If I wanted to fuck my way there, you mean."

She sat back on the bed, exasperated. "What makes you any better than me?"

"I'm not better than you."

"You have the most fascinating body, a naturally beautiful body, that I have ever seen. You're incredibly female without looking weak or cheap. But you are still just a body and a lovely face."

"I am more than that." That was what I wanted to prove. I was more than something men used.

"Marilyn Monroe thought so, too. Look where she ended up. Fucking presidents and their brothers. How much higher can you go? But she didn't get a part—even after she was a star—that she didn't have to fuck a producer to get first. What do you think she needed the alcohol and pills for? To forget that she was just a body to most of the world."

"I don't want to end up that way. I'd rather end up on my own terms, with my legs together. So I'm afraid I'll be staying married to Leo, for a while longer anyway."

"But you are planning to leave him?" Liza was speculative now.

"Yes. I'd venture to say that he guesses I'll try." If I was dead he'd have no reason to hurt Dina. It sounded insane—it *was* insane—to think in those terms, but Leo was inhuman in his love of cruelty.

She regarded me narrowly and said in a low tone, "I'll help you if I can, if he won't find out." She cracked a lopsided smile, the first genuine expression I'd ever seen from her. "Besides, if I can convince you I'm an ally and you do hit the big time, maybe it's you I'll leech on to. I don't change my goals, but my plans are flexible."

Leo was right. Liza was strong, very strong, born with steel for a spine and tempered by the world we lived in. "I'll remember," I said. "But I don't think you can help."

She stood, and her hands stroked my cheeks lightly. "I wish..."

She sighed and then left me to reach wearily for the eyebrow tweezers. That someone understood, even a little, what my life was like should have made me happy. But I felt even more depressed.

My future plans now depended entirely on what Leo planned for Dina and what it would take for me to spare her from his malice.

Away from the building, and with a huge quantity of eggs and toast in her, Dina felt rationality return. She'd been busy plotting how she would kidnap Christa, get her out of the city somehow, until she came to her senses over a third cup of coffee.

None of her wild plans would work. She had the chutzpah of a potato when it came to intrigue. She'd look like a nut case, and she could kiss her partnership, her reputation, the work of the past decade, good-bye.

Considering having a muffin, she decided it was all just a weird fantasy, some story her mother had told her when she was young, and she was remembering it, just like she remembered her mother's warnings about the gift she would inherit and the debt she had to pay. Unfinished business, her mother had said.

At the time her mother had first spoken about gifts and green, Dina had been too busy holding back her grief to listen closely. Now it seemed like the wanderings of a woman on too many painkillers. Depleted, emotionally strung out and sitting in the freezing cold of an empty building had made her hallucinate and recall her mother's dying words.

The muffin consumed and her stomach finally saying she'd had enough, she decided it was all madness. She was going to go home, take a nap, maybe do some of the reading she'd brought from the office—since she'd sworn she would not go to the office this weekend—and then take a long, hot bath before dressing for George's party. She was the guest of honor, after all, as the new partner. She would do him proud.

She left the diner to discover a morning drizzle. No umbrella as usual, but she didn't care. She'd just given her address when, to her surprise, the cab driver excitedly pushed open the dividing window.

"It's you! Like fate."

"I'm sorry?" Dina stared at the man, then abruptly recalled his face.

"You remember. I did what you said, and didn't get that fare. The cabbie who did, they tried to rob him. But he has gun and they run away. I don't have gun and there's no telling what they would have done." His excited gaze met hers in the rear view mirror. "You are psychic!"

"No, I'm not really—"

"I thank you always. My mother thank you always. My wife thank you always. My two babies thank you always. We pray for you, all family."

Well, Dina thought, it wasn't as if she couldn't use positive prayers. It couldn't possibly be real, she started to tell herself, but a whisper of her mother's voice asked what more proof she wanted. "I'm glad you were safe and the other cabbie too."

"You get idea for lottery numbers, you share, yes?" He whisked them along Central Park West.

"I don't think it works that way." She knew she should feel frightened and uncertain but instead she felt strong. She was Green. She fought back a giggle. Was this some kind of Faustian choice? If sanity wasn't working, she should opt for insanity?

"Forgive me, forgive me. I ask for too much good fortune."

He was still chattering when Dina got out of the cab. He refused her money. "I repay good fortune this way, maybe then I get more."

"Now that," Dina said, "is the way it's supposed to work. But here, if not for the meter, then for your babies so they'll pray for me more. I need all the prayers I can get." She pressed the bills into his hand and waved him away, cheered and energized by the encounter.

She was Green. Mad as a hatter, but Green.

Staring at herself in the bathroom mirror, haggard eyes and all, she thought she might be Green, but she still had a party to get ready for. George deserved her best and it was going to take a chunk of time to get there. She ought to have scheduled what Christa referred to as "a refurbishing" but her plain old moisturizer was going to have to do.

She soaked in the bath, aware that she had no idea what she was going to do about Christa and Goranson, but she was Green, wasn't she?

"Well, mom," she said to the shampoo bottle, "I'm waiting for a sign. It's your turn."

George called just after she finished painting her final toenail. "I hope you don't mind, but I invited Goranson to the party tonight."

"Ugh, George, why? You know how I feel about the guy."

"Because it was the only way I thought I could get Christa there as well. I made him promise she would attend so I could inflate my ego."

Dina didn't know what to say. She'd mentioned Christa to George, but she thought she'd been closed about her feelings. "You have incredible instincts."

"I saw your face last night, and hers. And I know people."

"Well, I was planning to put on the party duds anyway. I just want you to know that I bought this dress for you."

"But she'll enjoy it, I take it?"

"I certainly hope so. And George, I don't think Goranson is a jerk just because of Christa. He's a jerk."

"I also saw his face last night. He reminded me of the kind of guy who'd kill his own hamster and then want to take yours."

Remembering the woman in the club Goranson had taken her to, she wasn't sure it was hamsters that Goranson liked to torture. "We made him rich and it didn't hurt our pockets any."

"That's business."

She knew that, but it still pained her. She could do better with her talents than that. "Maybe we could endow some university's business department with a chair for ethical studies and doing business with bastards."

He chuckled and hung up, leaving Dina to wonder how she could use this unexpected opportunity to see Christa again.

It wasn't until she was leaving, putting a lipstick and some cash in her evening bag, that she had a nearly irresistible urge to go back to the building. There was more she could learn, but there was not enough time, she told herself.

It is time, a voice inside her head whispered.

Maybe she could do the second best thing. She snipped a leaf from the growing plant on the windowsill and filled a Ziploc with cornmeal. As she tossed in a few packets of takeout salt, she shook her head. This was crazy, she thought. So what else was new? She was Green, and crazy came with the territory, it seemed.

She was at the apartment door when thoughts not quite her own made her go back to the bedroom for her mother's dreamcatcher. It just fit in the slender bag, and when she left the apartment she had the preposterous feeling of being girded for battle.

Rahdonee felt her eyes straining to find some light, but there was none. She closed them again and concentrated for a moment on the smell of this place. Dank, of the earth.

Was she even alive? Was she waiting for the Great Mother to return her to the Wheel of Life?

She found she could move her arms, and she gingerly felt about her. Her fingertips encountered dirt, a thin web of root, a sleepy earthworm. She was not dead. She was alive and still with creatures of the Great Mother.

After that, where she was didn't concern her as much as the

growing pain of her wounds. She had been tended and bandages had been wrapped around her upper chest where most of the musket shot had struck her. She would live, and life was always to be treasured.

She woke some time later much clearer in mind, but still in absolute darkness. It was obvious that the men who had shot her had pulled her from the river, and she was most likely the prisoner of the demon preacher. The remainder of her life would probably be short and painful. She did not fear death, but the Great Mother would not begrudge her fearing the manner of it. Her death would be in such a way as to be of most use to the preacher.

Christabel. With a gasp of horror, she realized that her failure to escape him had given the preacher what he needed to force Christabel to do his bidding.

She clutched the dirt and made herself rise and explore the cell with eyes closed and fingers taking in every nook and cranny. The walls held echoes of suffering and despair, and she could not prevent these sensations from depressing her further. When she encountered several pairs of dangling manacles set in the wall higher than her shoulders, she understood. This was one of the places the traders kept their human cargoes before selling them at auction. There was no escape; these white men knew how to protect their property.

She would not get stronger without food, and the idea of toileting herself in the same place where she would sleep was repugnant. She could feel herself fighting off the lingering anguish held in the walls. It was draining her as surely as her wounds and lack of food.

She settled herself in a corner and reminded herself that her people were safe, and she tried to let that knowledge help her spirit float upward. She would not give the preacher the satisfaction of seeing her weep. In fact, the sooner he dispensed with her life, the less damage he would do to Christabel in the meantime.

What wickedness could wrench love to make it the source of despair? She had known he was evil, and yet she had delivered herself into his hands, to be his weapon against the woman she loved. Stupid, she had been stupid and naive. Love did not guarantee happiness or safety, and just because she was Green did not mean she could not be someone else's tool for evil.

There was no way to tell the passing of time without light, so she was left alone with her foolish pride, her anguished love, and the certain knowledge that when she next saw the sky it would be for the last time.

Chapter 15

Just another cocktail party, but I was grateful at least that it was not in a hotel where the press could follow us. Leo told me to wear the latest in his line of little black dresses designed for me, and I suspected the lead feeling inside me showed in my face. In fact, there was no sign of press when our limo arrived in front of the palatial Central Park West apartment building. A liveried bellman helped me out while Leo looked around him with disdain.

"I thought there would be press." He groused about it as we went to the elevator. "There's no point in going if it's not a PR opportunity." He glanced at me, his usual smugness turned up tenfold. "Well, something might come of it."

We took the elevator to the top floor, and it opened into the foyer of an elegant apartment with parquet floors and rich tapestries on the walls—a touch of the medieval. The view of Central Park could almost make me forget how many people were crammed onto this small island. A man turned toward us, and I recognized him from the fashion show—Dina's boss.

Leo tucked my shaking arm more tightly against his ribs. Of course he hadn't wanted to give me time to prepare. I knew my composure wouldn't hold when I faced Dina.

I extricated my arm to shake hands with George Berkeley. He admired my dress, complimenting Leo's design, then sweetly added, "And of course, Christa, you could wear a brown paper bag and give this old heart of mine a lift any day of the week. Let me introduce you to some special people."

I laughed politely and put my arm through his, forcing Leo to step back out of politeness. I could feel his gaze boring into my bare back as George led me away from him. I had no idea if his separating me from Leo was deliberate, but I could almost love him for doing it so adroitly.

"I am so glad you came this evening," he went on. "Dina told me some time ago that you liked modern art. I want to show you something."

He stopped to chat in various groups, introducing me as we went. Away from Leo's clutches I found everyone friendlier than I had hoped, and while it was obvious George was enjoying having me on his arm, he wasn't showing me off like a fancy bauble, but as he would any woman who had earned his respect. I wondered how I had earned his.

There were several people in the opulent library, and George scolded them for talking shop. He touched a switch, and an overhead spotlight illuminated a painting. It was so unexpected that I gasped. A Chagall, a real one. Not large, but full of his vibrant color. *The Circus Dancers*.

"Get closer," George urged. "Dina said he was your favorite."

I wanted to crawl into the yellow and green landscape of the brilliant circus world. The blues made me want to fly.

I turned to George with a grin, and he stepped back abruptly.

"I'm sorry," I said, realizing I'd discomfited him somehow. I wasn't doing *it* or anything.

"No—many pardons, Christa. I've seen your face in so many photographs and never realized that you weren't really smiling."

"It's just haughty model smiling in the pictures," I said, honestly.

"Have you thought of going into movies or television? When you smile like that, the entire world would smile with you, you know."

"I'm not sure I have the talent for it," I sidestepped. "Thank you for letting me see this."

"Slip back in any time you like. I'll leave the light on."

Over George's shoulder, a man said, "I didn't know you collected art, George."

George turned to make small talk with the newcomer, and I excused myself after a few minutes. To my surprise, as I made my way to the bar, several people drew me into their groups, asking my opinion about plays and movies. I was used to people giving way, of thinking me too beautiful to have a brain in my head. But that was when I was with Leo or other models. For just a few minutes I felt like an ordinary career woman who could be talked to instead of stared at. The sensation was both novel and nourishing.

I'd only ever before felt this way with Dina and as the feeling grew I knew my mother had never felt this way, nor her mother, nor any woman for who knows how many generations. More than a body, I felt like a whole human being.

I was astonished by how good it felt. In some ways, it was as good as the touch of Dina's hands.

I was so full of my high spirits that I didn't even realize when Dina entered. Someone said, "Wow," and everyone turned around.

I'd never seen her with her hair down. It fell halfway down her back, ending in large curls. Her vibrant green cocktail sheath was the color of her eyes, and it clung to her in places where I had rested my head, where I had kissed her and enjoyed the softness of her skin.

She had never seemed so tall, but then I'd never seen her in real heels before. George was greeting her, telling her enthusiastically that she was going to certainly liven up the partner's photograph in the annual report.

She hugged him, and over his shoulder her eyes met mine, as

if she'd known I was there from the moment she entered. She gave me such a look of love and pride that I couldn't help but respond. For that moment, Leo did not exist.

She was walking directly toward me. Eyes were still on her, and they followed her path to me. Her eyes asked permission; mine gave it. To have this moment was something I'd never dreamed of. Part of me accepted that we did not have a future beyond tonight. No doubt it was the selfish part of me that added, "So why not have tonight? One night is more than you ever dreamed possible."

She inclined her head, and I raised my mouth to hers for a short, but definitely intimate kiss. "I'm so glad you're here," she said after, loud enough for everyone nearby to hear. "Now we can plan what we're going to do tomorrow."

I felt the recognition ripple through the room. Everyone there understood that Dina and I were lovers. Then I remembered Leo, but even then I didn't care. I was within the aura of her strength, and nothing could hurt me.

Dina was not going to leave my side, that was clear. Our conversational group shifted and changed, with people from Dina's company, as well as major clients, congratulating her on her partnership. I overheard two younger men muttering that they supposed Dina wasn't sleeping with George after all. Leo never came near us.

"Christa, this is Jeff, the wonderful assistant who did so much of the work on the IPO." Dina put her hand on my back to turn me his way, and a delicious thrill ran through me. I shook his hand and then his wife's, and answered her breathless questions about what a model's life was like.

The evening turned into a shimmering kaleidoscope of smiling faces and laughter. When the crowd began to thin, George put on big band music and Dina took me into her arms and we swayed together, my heart beating in time to hers.

It was beyond any conception of happiness I'd ever had. I wanted the night to last forever. Tomorrow might be all the more terrible for the beauty of this night, but at least I would have the memory of her love.

Christabel could not focus her eyes. The light from the fire danced. She heard the doctor's voice, then Mr. Albright's. She could not make her mouth form words.

When she heard *his* voice she wanted to scream, but could only gurgle.

"I found them thus. I've been concerned about the mother's stability since the funeral. I suspected alcohol, but never thought she would harm her own daughter."

"I'd not have thought a woman could do it," the doctor said. "I've never known one who did."

Mr. Albright grunted, and then there was the cold clink of metal falling to the ground. "It's sharp enough."

"Then there's no question," the doctor said. "I'll prepare the body for a quick burial. There can't be a service."

"No, of course not," the preacher said. "A suicide cannot be mourned. But I will say a few words now, I owe the family that much."

"Of course, Reverend. I'll get the stretcher." Mr. Albright left the room with him, offering to help.

A shadow fell between her and the fire, and she opened her eyes again.

He was kneeling over her mother's prostrate form. He dipped a fingertip into the dark pool around her mother's hips, and he smiled.

She made a choking, gagging sound—it was all she could do. He turned to look at her.

"There are better and worse ways to die. This was a better way."

There was no stopping his evil smile. Murderer, she wanted to scream.

"When the poppy syrup I gave you wears off, I want only one sentence out of your mouth. If you say it, I will spare the witch's life. If you don't, I'll see her dead, and it won't be quick like this.

It's your choice." He dipped his finger again in her mother's blood. "You understand that I can do it?"

After a moment he nodded, finding sufficient terror in her expression. "What you will say is, 'I beg of you, save me by making me your wife.' Will you remember that? I want you to say that and nothing else."

He stroked her hair in a parody of fatherly concern. "You have no way of understanding what I can do. It is easy to use a knife, not so hard to make a team of horses go mad." He let that sink in. "I've gone to a lot of trouble to bring you begging to my bed. It would not take much effort to get people thinking of fire."

She couldn't roll over to vomit, but when he realized she was being sick, he pushed her away from him, onto her side. The pain in her ribs made her nearly faint again, and she could only let the bile trickle onto the floor.

He whispered into her ear, "We shall have many children, you and I. The boys will be like me. And all the girls like you." He stood up. "I think she's realized what has happened," he said to the returning doctor. "You'll take good care of her, won't you?"

"Of course, but she has no family now, poor thing, just in England."

"God has shown me how His mercy can reclaim this lost child from the evil that took both her parents. In service to His word, as my wife."

The doctor was rolling her onto the stretcher when her revolted gaze took in Mr. Albright licking his lips.

She swam toward the darkness, wanting to get lost in it. She asked Rahdonee's Great Mother to let her die.

She was like an angel to hold. Dina breathed in Christa's unexpectedly light perfume. "Do you trust me?"

"Yes."

"We have to confront him, and I think I know where. If I explained it you would think I'm crazy." She let her hands explore Christa's bare back. Her dress was a black halter that covered her from her neck to her waist in the front but left her back completely bare. If the neck came undone... That didn't bear thinking about, not if she wanted to keep her composure. She wondered if Goranson had selected that dress because it did make it hard for Dina to concentrate on anything else.

"He won't let me go."

"That's not his decision anymore."

She sighed in Dina's ear. "What do we do?"

"All I know is that it's going to be his will against ours. Yours and mine. And if we're united, he can't win. Do you believe me?"

"I want to."

"You have to believe me. He wants us confused and not thinking. We can't let him turn us against each other. It's the only way we win."

"And if we win, what happens then?"

"Then, my love, you can go anywhere, do anything, be whatever you want."

"You make that sound so simple."

Dina shifted Christa so she could look into her face. "My mother came from a long line of, um, well—"

"Green."

Dina blinked in surprise and led Christa away from the dancing. "Let's go into the library. Did you see the Chagall?"

"Yes, but I'd love to see it again."

They met George coming out as they went in.

"Thank you," Dina said. "For...you know. It was kind of you."

"Kind?" George rubbed his chin. "Let me put it this way. You happy means me richer. It's that simple."

"Right." Dina gestured at the library door. "Now get out for a while."

"It's my home, you know."

"Yes, and we're just going to talk." She closed the library door in George's disbelieving face.

Christa was gazing at the Chagall. "When we went to the museum together and we looked at your favorite, I thought the green was like your eyes."

As unwilling as Dina was to believe in fanciful tales of destiny and debts and unfinished business, she had to admit that there were too many coincidences. She dreamed of a demon, and in her visions a demon wore Leonard Goranson's face, and she made love to a Christabel who was as full of life and joy as the Christa in front of the painting was full of doubt and fear. Maybe it was all some story her mother had told her, but then how did Christa know about the significance of *green*?

She was asking Christa to believe that if they faced Goranson together they would win. She needed to listen to her own advice, because if she didn't believe in herself, Goranson would exploit her doubts.

"My mother's last words to me were a hope that I would be the one to find green. Her mother told her to look for green. And so on back for a ways." Christa turned from the painting, tears trembling in her eyes. "I couldn't let myself hope. Because hoping things will get better means I have to accept the present as it is. Which means going through with the deal I made if I want to be around for when things get better. God, that doesn't make any sense."

"Tell me about it. About the deal you made with him." Dina drew Christa to the leather sofa, sitting close enough to touch her hand, but far enough to see every flicker of emotion in her face.

"It'll sound stupid."

"Believe me." Dina patted my hand. "Not many things seem stupid to me right now. How old were you when you met him?"

"Twenty-one, a little over four years ago. I'd been on my own for four years before that. My mom died...my mom killed herself when I was seventeen."

Dina tightened her fingers around Christa's. "I can't even imagine what that must have been like."

"I don't go a day without knowing why she did it, and what she felt. I remember, when I was little, that she was so beautiful. Would it be conceited to say she was more beautiful than I am now?"

"No, but I find it hard to believe."

"She was. You have to understand, Dina. Women in my family don't live long. They marry badly. They get pregnant early, and they die. My mother was an old one—the ancient age of thirty-five. Her mother died in a back-alley abortion. One aunt died of pneumonia, the other was killed by her husband. Her grandmother died in childbirth, and if I remember it all, her great grandmother died in an opium den. And without exception they were all beautiful in their youth, but all of them at one point in their lives got on their back to survive. And when they did that, it was all over."

Dina wiped away the tear that trickled down Christa's cheek. Her mother had been nearly eighty when she died, after a long, useful life trying to make life better for others. They'd called her the Saint of the Bowery. Her grandmother had almost made it to ninety, a fascinating woman who had drawn landscapes in chalk and taught Dina to love art. Both had had adoring, loving husbands they had outlived by a number of years. Dina hardly remembered her father, in fact.

"I'm the only child of a doomed line of women," Christa was saying. "And when my mother died I told myself, this is it. This is the end of the line. There aren't going to be any more victims. I'm the last one. And I'll decide exactly what kind of victim I'll be. More than anything I wanted to be immortal, remembered for something. I'm sure that none of the men who used my mother even remembers her."

"And so Goranson is making you immortal as a supermodel."

Christa was nodding. "Leo was the only opportunity that came my way that didn't require me to lie down. How bad could it be, I thought. I agreed to his terms. He would put my face on at least six magazines—big magazines."

"Like *Vogue*, next week."

"That's number one. Numbers two through five will be done by fall. I'm sure number six will happen soon after that."

"And your end of the bargain?"

"I go to bed with him, willingly, and I give him a child." Christa's lips trembled before curving slightly. "But, you see, the funny part is, I'm not going to do it. He doesn't know that. My plan was to jump off a bridge or walk in front of a bus as soon as I had my measure of immortality and my tragic, untimely death would only add to it. I'd get the last laugh, so to speak."

Dina whispered, "And now?"

"Now there's you. And I've also come to accept that he's not an ordinary man. He thrives on the pain and inconvenience and stress he gives others. There have been models he fed on, like sucking them dry." Her lower lip trembled slightly as she took a deep breath. "I'll sound crazy, and I didn't want to see it that they were real, the things he did. He'd belittle and berate the new girls and destroy their confidence, and he'd laugh about it and call them weak. One girl got so distraught about her weight that she started...cutting off parts of herself. First her hair. The one day she showed up missing a toe. Leo said he was going to take her home."

Dina wanted to put her arms around Christa to quell the shudder than ran through her, but their bodies were already so close that Dina was finding it distracting. Distraction could be fatal. "What did he do?"

"He only told me about it. When she bled to death that night I'm not sure it was an accident. I know he was there. He just sat there and let her die. He told the police he was with me and how shocked and saddened we all were. It sounds so crazy—

"I believe you. There's a simple word for him—*evil*."

"And that's why he wanted us to be together. Wanted me to get under your skin, into your bed, so that he could use hurting me as a way to force you to do—I don't know what. But something that would destroy you in the end. Something that would take away your Green and give him more power."

Firmly, she repeated, "He can't hurt us if we face him together."

"I want to believe you. But what I know is that if I have a choice between letting him hurt you and giving him what he wants, he can have it. He can have me. I don't care. You are all that matters to me."

"That's how he wins. Christa, listen to me." Dina cupped her face. "You were right. It ends here. You've been looking for the Green, and maybe I am it. Maybe my mother was right and I have some unfinished business. But it can't end here if you agree to sacrifice yourself. I am not worth more than you."

"I am so afraid," she whispered.

Dina kissed the salty cheeks and lost herself in the passion of Christa's mouth. She heard the rustle of tree branches in the wind and the clicking of crickets.

Christa undid the collar of her dress, and bared herself in a single motion. "Please."

Dina's head swam. She could not help herself. Her teeth grazed the lush perfection of Christa's breasts, and she dreamed of losing herself between Christa's thighs.

A warning note sounded in her mind, finally, and she raised her head. "We can't do this here," she said, her voice like gravel.

"Don't stop on my account. After all, she's only my wife."

Christa gasped and covered herself, while Dina tried to shake the lethargy of passion. She cleared her throat. "You and I have some unfinished business."

"That we do," Leonard said. "And I think we'd better tend to it this evening. I was going to wait until tomorrow evening, but this is a golden opportunity. I think you're in the right frame of mind."

Christa was shaking all over, and she seemed unable to make her eyes look anywhere except Goranson.

"What on earth do you think I'm going to do with you at this hour?"

"Anything I want, darling Dina. First, you're going to take a little ride with my darling wife and me. The limo is waiting downstairs."

He gestured at Christa, and she rose shakily, refastening her collar. "You've done well." He held out his hand and Christa took it. "You see," he said to Dina, "she is completely mine. If you want

161

her to be healthy, you will cooperate."

Dina felt the pressure of his malice. "Let me say good night to George," she said, with great resignation. She was afraid, and she let some of it show.

"Of course. You wouldn't want your boss to know you were in the process of seducing the woman married to a client, now would you? We will finish our business this evening," he said smugly.

Dina pondered how long it would take to bash his head in with one of George's heavy bookends. A waste of thought, but picturing him dead on the floor helped her conquer some of her fury.

She did not know what he wanted her to do, but she was ready to do whatever it took to put an end to his cruelty. But not with a blunt object. "And I'll just get my purse."

Chapter 16

When food and water came it was after dark, but even then the dim light of a sputtering torch blinded Rahdonee. She knew who brought it; his presence had the stink of pestilence.

Through her watering eyes she saw where the opening was and that it was more than double her height. He lowered a bucket.

"Empty it now or I'll pull it back up and you can just get hungrier."

Defiance over food and water would be foolish. She found a bowl of some sort of steaming grain and a flask of water. Both containers were leather and impossible to make into weapons to turn on him—or herself.

"May I keep the bucket for my...waste?"

He was silent, then barked, "Untie it then."

A kindness, but no doubt his reasons had more to do with cleaning up after she left this place than wanting her to find any comfort. She untied the rope and found the bucket heavier than she had thought. If she threw it, she might hit him. But it would not get her out of this hole.

He thrust the torch into the opening, and she fell back, blinded again.

"Her mother has died unexpectedly. Took her own life."

She knew immediately of whom he spoke, and her heart ached for Christabel and for her mother.

"At least that's what the doctor says. She knows differently."

Her vision was clearing, and she found herself in the same unrelenting darkness as he lowered the door over the opening. "She understands that you will also die if she does not please me."

"No," she breathed, unprepared for the degree of the preacher's ruthless evil.

"Your life is my wedding gift to her, but we won't be inviting you to the ceremony. You understand, I'm sure. I'd almost want you there for the wedding night, to see how she enjoys her new life with me. Lie in this hole, witch, and think of it."

The door dropped into place, and she heard a bolt being shot.

For a long while she could not bring herself to eat. Layered on the terror and suffering of the people brought to the island to be bought and sold was the image of his leering face. The walls echoed with Christabel's crying.

Bitsy Albright held her hand, though her touch was of no comfort. "We'll pin up one of mother's dresses for you," she was saying. "You're too big for mine, and besides it wouldn't be right for you to wear mine when I haven't worn it yet." She sighed. "Tom is going to have ever so much money when his father dies, but I wish he was as handsome as the Reverend."

Christabel didn't respond. She would not speak.

"You're so lucky. You certainly couldn't marry into a noble family, but a prince of the Church is the next best thing. Mother says that's not what preachers want, to be princes of the Church and all, but I think of him that way. He is so strong, and so handsome."

Christabel opened her eyes and fixed her horrified gaze on Bitsy. Bitsy's color was high.

"Now don't be jealous," Bitsy said in a whisper. "It was the best penance I've ever done. I told him about meeting that witch in the woods with you and he said I'd get infected, too, and he knew a way to make sure she was no longer witching me. It's not in the least wicked because he's a man of God, but he says mother and father wouldn't understand because they don't want to believe there's something so wicked walking among us. You are going to be so lucky. I'm sure Tom is not even half the man the Reverend is." She laughed, blushing more furiously.

Christabel turned her head to the wall and willed herself to silence. He described himself and told poor Bitsy he was talking about Rahdonee. She wanted to hate Bitsy but couldn't.

"Has she said anything?"

Bitsy jumped and let go of Christabel's hand. "No, ma. She's not crying as much, though."

"You've been good for her, I'm sure. I'll sit with her for a while."

Like Bitsy, Goody Albright talked of nothing but the wedding. "It's such a shame it has to be so simple, but given your circumstances, well, you can't celebrate as a bride should. He's so good to take you in. Did you know he caught that witch? But he says she can be cured and that God would find it merciful."

Christabel chanted "Rahdonee" in her mind to shut out the room, the future, everything. She willed herself to feel the sunlight on her skin, to hear the Sacred Tree dancing with the Wind God. Rahdonee's beautiful hair was a curtain around them, and the sunlight through the leaves tinted her skin the green of new corn.

How happy she had been in Rahdonee's arms, in her world. She would stay there now.

Rahdonee, she pleaded in her mind. Be safe, get away. Be safe. She could bear anything if she knew Rahdonee was alive.

The tendril of thought that caressed her mind was like water to her parched soul.

My love, do not cry for me.

Where are you?

That is not important. But Christabel gathered images of darkness, and her mind brushed against Rahdonee's growing despair. *My love, it is not important.*

I won't let him kill you.

You must not give in. Fight him. What happens to me isn't important. The Great Mother will give me her mercy. Do not give—

"Has she spoken?"

Christabel gasped and cowered from his gaze.

"No, Reverend," Goody Albright answered. "She was smiling a moment or two ago."

His grimace made Christabel think he knew why. He knew everything. She flattened herself against the wall behind the bed, the covers pulled up to her chin.

"It's as you said," Goody Albright went on. "She is frightened of your goodness. The evil taint that took her parents would take her, too."

"I cannot allow that," he said. "Christabel, you can be saved, if only you can ask for it."

Rahdonee was lying in darkness, in an evil place, slowly starving. She believed she was going to die, and Christabel knew she had the power to change that. She could make one good thing come of the evil this man had brought to her life. Was it such a high price to pay? She could run away, after, and find Rahdonee and her people.

She swallowed hard, then coughed. She stuttered at first, then managed to say clearly, "I beg of you, save me by making me your wife." She stared into his eyes, wanting to tell him that she had not forgotten his promise to spare Rahdonee.

For a moment his eyes glowed red, and she felt the horrible invasion of his will. Even after he left, his tiny smile of victory was burned in her mind.

The air was heavy with the scent of impending rain, and humid with the sweat of summer heat trapped by the clouds. Dina

166

ducked her head into the limo and wondered, for an irrelevant moment, if she should have brought an umbrella.

What would wet feet matter if she could manage to break this weird hold that Goranson had on Christa? She'd walk naked through a hundred storms if that was what it took.

Christa didn't look at Dina during the short ride to Fifty-fifth Street, while Goranson didn't look anywhere else. Dina wasted energy hiding her desire to squirm. Was it just force of personality, or something more? If she hadn't seen how lightning fast the change in Christa was, she might have thought it was drugs, but it was as if he could effortlessly turn a light off inside Christa. Dina had no idea how to turn it back on.

"Why here?" Dina already knew, but she was curious what Goranson would say.

"I waited for years for this building to come on the market. It has a special nostalgia for me." He stopped briefly at the large table that held the architect's model, taking a slender book from a drawer. "Let's go downstairs, shall we?"

Christa didn't move. She shook all over for a moment, then said clearly, "No."

"Move," he ordered.

Christa whispered, "No."

His response was immediate and unexpected—Dina staggered from his unchecked backhand. Stars danced in her vision. While she gasped and tried to snap out of the shock, he seized Christa and spun her so one hand clamped on her throat and the other bent an arm so sharply Dina expected to hear it pop. She wanted to attack him but this conflict wouldn't be won that way. She realized, only then, that she wasn't prepared to kill him, but watching him twist Christa's arm she was starting to comprehend how people are driven to kill. The side of her face throbbed— she'd never been struck before in her life, but if he thought that would make her afraid of him, he was wrong.

"Neither of you understands the stakes. I don't care which of you I hurt, I just know that it doesn't matter. You'll cooperate because if you don't I'll hurt the other one."

Christa sobbed, "I'll go, I'll go."

Dina wasn't prepared for the wrenching she felt at Christa's distress. Damn it, she wasn't afraid of him for her own sake, but for Christa's. He'd deftly separated them and now played their pain against each other.

She heard herself say, "All right, all right, let go of her. You win," from far away. She'd been a fool thinking he wasn't dangerous, thinking this was just an elaborate mind game. For the first time in her life she wanted a gun. What had she been thinking, delivering them both so willingly into his control?

He let go of Christa by pushing her toward the door. She caught herself on the jamb at the top of the first set of stairs, then made her way down them, still sobbing. Goranson sketched a parody of a gentlemanly after-you gesture, and Dina preceded him down the stairs.

As she navigated the steps, she cursed herself for being a fool, for telling Christa not to sacrifice herself when, at the first sign of Christa's tears, she had caved just as quickly.

As they crossed the first basement toward the second flight of stairs, Dina found herself dipping her fingertips stealthily into her purse. She crushed the packets of takeout salt in her hand. Christa went first down the stairs, but when Goranson gestured that she should go second, Dina drew back. They scuffled briefly at the top of the landing, giving Dina just enough time to scatter the salt behind both of them and across the doorway.

He shoved her into the wall and then down the stairs. She caught herself before she fell all the way, but lost one shoe in the process. Just as well, she thought. She was not going to be at the mercy of high heels. She picked up the fallen shoe at the bottom of the stairs, and started to limp across the room. She removed the other shoe, clutching them both to her chest as if she was sorry she wasn't wearing them.

Christa was supporting herself against the wall near where the roots were curling through. Her teeth chattered. "I'm going to be sick, Leo."

"I don't care."

"What is it you want from me?" Dina lifted her chin. "The stock price is set, there's nothing I can do about it. There's no more money from the investors."

His charming and cruel mouth curved into amusement. "Even now, you don't understand, do you? This is not about money."

The weak light flickered, then flattened, giving Goranson an enormous shadow. Dina was suddenly aware of the nauseating smell from her nightmare, and she heard the chittering of the demon.

She dropped her purse and shoes and covered her ears as a burst of pressure, like an underwater dive, shot pain through her temples.

Goranson looked like a bad special effect from a Stephen King movie. His eyes glowed red, and his throat bubbled with a menacing laugh meant to frighten her. It did. When was she going to get that there were worse things than dying?

"I have not fed this well in three hundred years," he said. "Both of you at the same time, just as it was then. Absolutely delicious. Your stupidity is almost as delectable as your spirit."

He advanced on Dina, and the pain in her head intensified to the point of narrowing her vision until all she saw was his face.

"She's so easy to drain, but she's always available. Like mother, like daughter. But you gave her an extra dash of defiance that was wonderful to take away again. So thank you, darling Dina. That was an unexpected pleasure."

He turned from her, leaving her gasping as some of the pain receded. He squatted in front of Christa, who had crumpled to her knees, and opened the small volume he'd taken from the table. "It's time for you to know all. Your family album, Christabel. Look."

What Dina could see of the pictures looked like shot after shot of Christa, but with each page the dresses grew more old-fashioned. The pictures gave way to sketches, each the image of Christa. The last was a sketch of Christa in a simple colonial gown.

"On the day of our very first wedding," he said.

Christa looked at him, dazed.

He moved his hands so quickly Dina couldn't follow the motions. A flicker of light, and he had another photograph in his hands. "And this is our next wedding. You're a beautiful bride. We will have many children. The boys will all be like me, and the girls just like you. Look at the picture."

"Don't do it, Christa."

"You shut up!" He gestured casually at her, and Dina put both hands to her choking throat. She fell to her knees, fighting for air.

Christa glanced back and forth between them. Finally, she cried out, "Stop it, Leo! I'll do it!"

Dina could breathe in the next instant. She scrabbled for her purse, managed to get the Ziploc bag open and let the cornmeal scatter from her fingertips as she rose to her feet.

Christa was looking at the picture, her jaw slack.

Dina slung the bag as hard as she could, dusting its contents onto Goranson and Christa, then on herself.

Goranson roared with rage as he lunged at her, but Dina got to the wall first. Without hesitation she plunged up to her elbows in the quivering roots.

For you...

Rahdonee woke from the nightmare in a sweat of terror. They were visions too horrifying to contemplate. Christabel standing with the demon preacher in his church, Christabel letting him put the binding ring on her finger.

Then later, Christabel undressing and slipping white-faced between coarse sheets, repeating what he told her to say, that she was ready, that she wanted him to come to their bed, that she wanted him.

Sickening, it was foul and wrong and Rahdonee wept in the dark, never having felt so far from the Great Mother, so far from love.

She ached at Christabel's relief when he turned her away from him, pressing her face into the pillows. Not to have to look at him—it was easier to pretend it wasn't happening.

For you...

It was no nightmare, and Rahdonee wailed to the Great Mother, unable to bear the burden of Christabel's sacrifice, and knowing in her heart that it was for nothing.

"The house is yours to tend now." He was dressed already.

Christabel made herself get out of bed, though each motion was an agony. Her thighs and arms screamed with pain and her face and jaw felt swollen.

She made him a breakfast of oats and cream while he watched her every move. He ate in silence and looked at her in such a way that she trembled with fear.

"I've no doubt that no one expects newlyweds to be out and about so early. I'd dally with you for the morning if I didn't have so much to do today." He rose. "Come here, my wife."

She went, and kissed him when he asked.

"When will you let her go?" She had been afraid to ask, and she was more afraid still. But for the sake of her sanity, she needed to know how long she had to endure.

"This evening," he said. "You'll see her then."

I smoothed the picture of my mother. I'd never seen it before. She hadn't liked her picture taken.

Was the next page my mother's mother? And her mother's mother?

One long line of victims. We all had the same empty eyes.

Dina's cry of pain made me look up. I wanted desperately to help her, but I was frozen in place. Leo was trying to pull her away from the wall. He had her by the hair, but she wouldn't let go.

Then Leo made a grab for one of her arms, which was lost in the roots and the crack in the wall. And then the roots were around Leo's arm, and he couldn't get free.

He screamed.

I wanted to laugh. Then I felt stinging in my arms, as if the roots that now bound him bound me as well.

Chapter 17

When the demon preacher told her she could climb the ladder to freedom, Rahdonee didn't believe him. But she climbed into the night air because dying under the sky was better than dying in the black hole he'd kept her in. The moonlight and his torch dazzled her eyes.

The wind nearly knocked her off her feet, then she heard weeping. "Christabel."

"I'm sorry," she managed through her tears.

"What a tender reunion." He thrust his torch into the air, waving it three times. "Remember, my wife, that I set her free."

The ground rumbled, and Christabel turned in horror. "Oh my God! My God! Run!" She threw herself on the preacher and nearly succeeded in knocking him to the ground before he shoved her into the dirt.

Rahdonee's eyes wouldn't focus on the clusters of stars rushing toward her. Only when they were upon her did she realize they were torches carried by stony-faced Puritans. The ground shook under the tread of their relentless feet.

It was too late to run, and her weakened body could not have gone more than a few steps before they caught her. She shrank back when a man stepped forward with manacles.

With a triumphant grin, the preacher said, "It's for your own good, Christabel. She's set a spell on you, and we're all the family you have now." He gestured at Rahdonee, and when she didn't turn around, two other men forced her to allow the fastening of heavy irons to her wrists.

"Don't you dare to touch me yourself?" Rahdonee drew herself up to her full height so she could look down on him. The chain between her wrists was so short she could not relax her arms. "It is always others who do your evil bidding, and they are the ones whose souls will bear the burden."

He only smiled, cool and calm. "You cannot challenge me, witch. You cannot win."

She returned his smile even though her heart was breaking at the sound of Christabel's unchecked sobbing. "You presume we mean the same thing by winning."

"I have her." He gestured at Christabel's crumpled form. "I think that's all that matters to you."

She would not let him see that he spoke the truth. She opened her mouth to make a scathing reply, but a voice in the crowd broke her concentration.

"Death to the witch!" The cry was taken up by more and more voices, but the only thing Rahdonee cared about was the sharp gasp Christabel made when the preacher yanked her to her feet.

They prodded her into the street from behind the auctioneer's platform, and onward through the town. The moon rose and the crowd grew. When they passed through the town gates, she realized with horror where they were taking her to die.

Goranson's arm was bleeding where the roots had attached to him, and Dina did not care that he still had a grip on her hair. An unearthly shriek split the air and the demon—real, not nightmare—was biting at the roots to free him.

She had nothing with which to fight the demon. She gave up her own hold on the roots to grab Goranson's other arm in an attempt to bring it into contact with the roots as well. Whatever they were, they hurt him and he deserved the pain.

The demon raised its bloody mouth and bared its teeth. It lunged into the space she pushed herself from, and then twisted to launch itself on her as she scrabbled on the floor.

It was almost upon her, and she spun around, holding her mother's dreamcatcher over her heart like a shield.

The creature's impact on the spiderlike web brought another shriek, this time of pain, not fury. The heat burned Dina's hands, and a brilliant flash of light blinded her. She choked on sulfur fumes, and then, blessedly, the creature's shrieking ended in a sound like the breaking of a thousand mirrors.

She dropped the ruined dreamcatcher, unable to believe that the demon was gone, that it had even existed, nor that she was blistered to her elbows. She felt nothing where she was burned, and knew enough to tell that was a bad sign.

"Help me."

She stared numbly at Goranson. The roots had coiled around his chest, and his long leather jacket was growing slippery with his own blood.

Christa rocked in place, whimpering quietly, her eyes unseeing.

"If you don't help me, she'll never recover," Goranson gasped. "You've killed my companion. I'm going to grow old now. I'll die just like any mortal when the time comes. You've cost me eternity, isn't it enough?"

There was no light in Christa's eyes. They were nearly black with her wretchedness. What would it take to bring them back to life? Dina had been asking herself that question since the day they had met, and she didn't want to believe the answer had anything to do with him. Her eyes could not ignore, however, that Christa's shoulders were marked with red lines of distress, matching the pattern of the roots that held Goranson. His pain transferred somehow to Christa.

"I'll save her," Goranson choked. "But only if you save me."

She didn't believe him. "Christa, let's get out of here."

Christa made no sign of having heard her.

Moving slowly, not wanting to frighten her, Dina gently touched one shaking shoulder.

Christa shrank from the contact, her eyes still staring into some place of misery. Dina grasped more firmly and the helpless whimper Christa made cut into Dina's heart.

After a steadying breath, Dina made to slip one arm around Christa, planning to pick her up if necessary. She'd get her away from Goranson and that would break his spell. "I'm sorry, sweetheart, but I have to."

Christa shrieked and wrested herself from Dina's grasp. When Dina tried again Christa slapped away her hands before slumping to the ground in a fetal ball.

"I told you." Goranson's voice had taken on a bubbling edge. "Only I can save her."

She still didn't believe him. She didn't trust him. But she couldn't get Christa out of here without help and she wasn't leaving to summon it.

She had made so many mistakes and she was convinced this was another one, but what choice did she have? She reached out, closing her burned hands on the largest of the bloodstained roots over his chest.

When Rahdonee fell, someone was there to pick her up. Her eyes would not adapt to the light, and her arms bound behind her were useless for balance. Where she had once run like a deer without a false step, she stumbled, stubbed her toes, bloodied her knees, and fell heavily on her chest and shoulders.

Christabel's journey was equally harsh. Rahdonee heard her fall several times, only to be pulled back to her feet. She looked back at her as often as she could, wanting at least to try to say good-bye, but someone always prodded her with the butt of a musket to keep her moving.

They were halfway to the Sacred Tree when Rahdonee couldn't find the strength to stay standing. They pulled her to her feet, but she sagged.

"Get up," the preacher ordered. "You have no choice."

She would not let them march her to her own death so easily. She would make them carry her.

Christabel yelped, and the sound made Rahdonee's heart jump as sharply as the musket shot that had thrown her into the river.

"Get up." He dropped to the ground beside her and said in her ear, "These people aren't convinced that she can be saved from your spells."

"You call yourself a man of God." She panted, trying to catch her breath. "And you would subject me to Calvary? I have done you no harm."

"What an interesting comparison," he mocked. "You and Christ? I'll be happy to inform my followers that the witch compares herself to our Lord. Of course you haven't harmed me. What would be the pleasure in simple revenge on you? You," he whispered intently, "are a victim. And she will be mine forever because of you. Now, if you don't get up, I'll make sure she can't either. And the wolf pack might begin to think that we need to rid ourselves of both of you."

Rahdonee found the strength somewhere. She managed one foot in front of the other, too dizzy and blinded to travel more than a few steps before falling again. What energy she could spare went to silently pleading with Christabel to forgive her.

Chapter 18

At Dina's touch, the root curled away from Goranson's body. She looked down at Christa, who had not moved. Was she irrevocably linked to Goranson? If he died, would she? Impossible, but then none of this was possible. She gritted her teeth to stand the growing pain in her scorched hands, and touched another root. It curled away with a sigh Dina felt rather than heard.

"Hurry," he panted. "She's getting worse."

He had no honor. She had no way to force him to do as he promised. She left him, ignoring his gasp of pain. Let him suffer for once, she thought, as she bowed over Christa's huddled form. Hoping it wouldn't cause more pain, Dina briefly touched Christa's shoulder.

Her fingers came away bloody.

She gagged, unprepared for the sticky smell of it. Christa's shoulder was not cut. There was no wound there, only the red lines to match Goranson's. Dina brushed her fingers over the faint red lines on Christa's forearm and, again, her hand was coated with blood.

"Help me," he grated. "And I will release her. When she looked at the picture, we were joined. If I die, she dies."

She should call an ambulance, she should find a cop, call 9-1-1, do something sensible. But her senses were swimming with horror and indecision. Her throbbing hands made it hard to think clearly.

If she freed him, he would not help Christa. But if she didn't free him, Christa might die, too. Either way he would win.

From deep inside came the bitter question: *why does he always get to win?*

There were no choices. Nothing made sense. The world was upside down. None of this could be real, but here she was, caught between a desire for vengeance for crimes she didn't even understand and an abiding love that gave her glimpses of heaven.

She touched the roots one by one, wincing when her fingers bent even slightly. She left the largest for last. When he was free she scrambled away, putting herself between him and Christa.

He lurched to the floor with a groan.

She was shaking like a leaf, exhausted and frightened. She did not know what he would do next.

What he did surprised her, as always. Instead of attacking them, he simply ran for it. He bolted for the stairs and grimaced in amusement when she made no effort to follow him. At the top of the stairs he reached out one hand. "Good-bye, my dear wife. As for you, you were always a nuisance."

Dina felt the wave of his attack, and she put up her hands. The dreamcatcher was ruined and she had no shield or weapon now. She felt the tingle of something sour against her palms. There was a sizzle of green light. Then nothing.

"Damn you both," he cursed. He reached for the door.

His fingertips couldn't touch it. He tried to grasp the knob and kick the door. He seemed to come within an inch of it and no closer.

He turned amazed eyes on her. "She *was* a witch. And you are, too."

Unbidden words came to her lips. "Call it what you like. We will oppose you."

He snarled, "Well, then, let us finish now!" He vaulted the

banister.

Heart pounding with terror, Dina grabbed for her purse on the floor. She had one last weapon, as fragile as an eggshell, but as strong as life.

Not even a second before he grabbed her hair to yank her back, she joined the thickest curl of pale root dangling from the wall with the leaf that had rooted in the moonlight and sprouted at the touch of her hand.

The cracks around the roots surged with green lightning. Energy danced across Dina's body. She gasped for air, heard Christa scream, and then everything went black.

Only when they unbound her hands did she realize they were at the Sacred Tree. She thought she might have sensed its warmth, but she felt nothing but her own pain. Two men bore her up rough stairs. A gallows? There were worse ways to die. Hanging was at least quick.

When they bound her with her back to the tree, she was so glad that she missed the significance. Its loving sustenance welled up in her, and she lifted her face to the wind to make her last prayer to the Great Mother. The sky was low, heavy with clouds. She was puzzled and then she realized she had expected to see branches.

With a moan of despair she saw that the tree had been cut off just above her head. It lived still, its eternal serenity unchanged. Its spirit nourished her.

"I have tried to purify this witch, but walking in the path of our Lord has not wrenched the evil from her soul," the preacher shouted. "God has spoken! This is our answer to the evil in the heavens and our promise to any of her people who may ever dare to return to our lands. Let it begin!"

The mob roared. Christabel screamed, and her terror brought Rahdonee back to what was about to happen. This was not a gallows, not a whipping post.

Her unbelieving eyes watched them drag bundles of kindling

from the underbrush. They packed it under the platform she stood on and all around the tree.

Great Mother, no. Spare me this, give me your mercy.

The preacher lifted his torch, and the crowd fell silent. Their mindless hunger was already devouring her spirit.

Mercy, Mother of us all. Give me your gentle care, take me from this place now, before—

Just as she thought her plea for oblivion would be answered, Christabel shrieked again. The preacher had wrapped her hand around the torch and carried her bodily toward the kindling. She twisted, kicked, bucked, but he thrust the torch into the first bundle while her hand still grasped it. Then others darted forward with their torches. In moments the tree was circled with crackling flame.

Christabel was sobbing as if her heart and mind had forever broken. He tossed her on the ground like a used rag and grinned up at Rahdonee, his victory complete.

The first of the flames licked at the platform and smoke filled her lungs. Rain hissed into the rising inferno, but not enough to quench it.

Looking like the picture of concern, he lifted the unconscious Christabel into his arms. Only Rahdonee could see that the fire turned his eyes red. In a shattering flash of lightning, she saw his hand stroking Christabel's breast.

Thunder rumbled across the sky, and the rain turned into a torrent. The mob was driven back by the fury of the storm and Rahdonee's pulse matched the hammering of the rain.

The heat was building in spite of the downpour. The roar of the flames filled her ears. She licked the Sky God's tears from her parched lips, and lifted her face to let it cool her stinging cheeks.

I will survive this, even if it takes me eternity, and he shall find me in his nightmares. Great Mother, give me grace from this evil. Let me abide to see it quenched.

The tree felt warm at her back now. It, too, would not survive the inferno. She imagined she felt the sap, the tree's life blood, retreating into the roots, away from the heat, just as she longed to retreat.

All at once, it seemed very simple. She blinked. The world was green. One last look, nearly her last conscious thought, was for Christabel's lost spirit.

I shall find her again, she vowed.

I shall leave this shell. *He has not won.*

She was not there when the first flames touched her. Coolness surrounded her, and she followed the tree's retreat, sinking down into roots buried deep and wide. They tickled the River God, who welcomed her and offered a place to rest until the time came to awaken.

Christabel.

She rested.

GREEN   GREEN   green   green   green greengreengreengreen...

The exultant cry echoed from the walls. Dina struggled to regain consciousness, but a joy so fierce and a rage so implacable throbbed all around her, leaving her limp in the face of it.

The presence, the source of the calling, wasn't even paying attention to her. Goranson was choking, gasping for air, clawing at his throat. A sound like a helicopter beat inside Dina's head... and then calm.

Peace descended on her in a welcome wave. Oh, no wonder. She was in a small corner of her mind now, sheltered.

She surged to her feet and leaned over the choking man. Her voice rang like a thousand bells on the wind.

"More than death awaits you, preacher. More than pain. In my first life I would have been merciful, but I am no longer the daughter of the Great Mother. I am vengeance incarnate, and I will show you the mercy you showed us."

Dina saw it all then. He had stolen a thing of beauty, a product of a new and wild land. He'd satisfied his human lusts on her over and over again, throughout the centuries, while his demon companion feasted on her suffering.

Goranson was writhing on the floor, his body in spasms as if electrified.

Dina tried to form a warning to the new presence. Christa was showing signs of Goranson's distress, as if he pushed his pain onto her.

Green eyes bored into her own, they were her eyes, staring back at her, like a mirror. They tilted; there were a thousand eyes, and she knew everything and they knew everything.

The frenetic pounding eased and all the eyes blinked slowly. A different sound rose, laden with love. *Christabel…*

I heard a voice in my head. It was like a lullaby I'd forgotten I knew combined with the gentle tinkling of bells.

Christabel…come to me.

It wasn't Dina. It wasn't Leo. I answered, or part of me did. And then it was as if the part of me that was wounded, that he had hurt, rose out of me. I looked up at the shimmering white light, amazed that something so beautiful could have been inside me.

Come to me, beloved.

The voice seemed to be coming from Dina, even though her mouth didn't move. But then I saw the glowing emerald that rose out of her body, and it twined around my wounded self, green and white swirling.

They were dancing. They were laughing and crying. I heard it all in my head. I raised my arms, and my legs obeyed me. I rose to meet Dina's embrace. All that mattered was the kiss we shared, that *they* shared through us.

I was wrapped in green. It was no longer sanctuary. It was life itself. And I knew everything. I didn't want to leave the welcome warmth of Dina's arms, but…I knew everything.

Freedom wasn't something Leo could give me. I had to take it.

He was a wreck, but still his elemental force was unbroken. I could feel him trying to work his way back into my mind as I leaned over him.

I saw him clearly for the first time.

I saw all of his faces. An abusive john, a bumbling abortionist, a pharmacist giving poison instead of antibiotics. I went back in time until I stared into the red eyes of a preacher who had used an inferno to crush my spirit utterly.

I unsnapped the clasp on my dress and let it slip low enough for me to step out of. It represented his image of me, a temptation, an object to be lusted after, possessed, debased and thrown away.

I was no longer a victim. I would decide what kind of woman I was. I held the dress over his shuddering body and let it drop.

He let out a woof as if bricks had fallen on him. He gazed at me, astonished.

"Let it be your shroud," I said, and I turned my back on him forever.

My mother, my mothers, all my mothers who were me, I could hear their voices joined in relieved release, like the gentle rush of doves taking flight.

Dina slid back into her body as the presence left it. Off balance, she stumbled to the floor, adding another set of bruises to her aching knees. When the room stopped tipping to one side, she watched Christa walk toward her. She was nearly naked, and she moved like an Amazon warrior. Her eyes were lit like liquid amber, and they danced with celebration of freedom.

"Do you think anyone would notice me if I went out like this?"

Dina wanted to say she could hardly breathe for looking at Christa, and she was quite sure the rest of New York wouldn't be able to handle it either. But her mouth was too dry. She wasn't afraid, though her heart was pounding.

She felt like a lake begging a swan to alight on its warm surface. She found the energy to get up, one more time. Christa opened her arms and Dina wrapped herself in them, filling herself with the pure gladness of holding Christa. Green and white light danced around them, infusing the air with joy.

She remembered, nearly too late, that she shouldn't turn her back on Goranson. A roar like a wild animal spun Dina to face him. He had Christa's dress looped between his hands and made to catch Christa around the throat.

Dina screamed and snatched Christa from his path. She fell back as the air pulsated with an explosion of green light. Then Christa was dragging her away from Goranson.

"Leave him. We've got to get the hell out of here."

Dina sobbed with anger and frustration. "He's never going to leave us alone. He'll never—"

Christa's dress burst into flames as if someone had put a torch to it. He shrieked and tried to let go of it, but the fabric was melting and spreading like burning oil.

The voice rang urgently in Dina's mind. You must go. We faced his ultimate evil, and now he must face us.

At the top of the stairs she swept away the salt and the door opened easily. Christa pushed past her, but Dina had to look back. Whatever he was, she was her mother's daughter, and she couldn't just leave him. He'd die without medical attention.

Daughter of all of us, go.

Dina found herself outside the closed door with no awareness of having moved. She tried to turn the knob with her singed hands, but it was locked and suddenly too hot for her burns to bear touching.

She backed away from the door.

Christa said urgently, "Dina, we've got to get out of here. Please, darling, we must."

When she saw the fingers of smoke curling under the door she came to her senses. Dina hurried behind Christa up the stairs to the main floor, her nostrils suddenly filled with the acrid odor of smoke. Her skin tingled with heat, and her blistered hands throbbed with each step. For a moment she was bound to the tree, watching the flames come nearer.

Daughter, go. He did not win then. He does not win now.

Christa resourcefully stepped into a pair of filthy work overalls abandoned by one of the painters. Pulling Dina unrelentingly with her, they dashed out to the deserted street.

To Dina, the rain had never been so welcome. She raised her face to the cool drops and accepted the gift of the Sky God.

A see-nothing, say-nothing cab driver didn't even give them a second glance as he bore them away.

"Bella! Bella! One more!"

George Berkeley leaned into the microphone. "If you want to hear what Christabel has to say, stop blinding her."

The flashbulbs continued to pop for a few more moments before they subsided.

I stepped up to the microphone, cleared my throat and read what George and I had carefully written out.

"I was as shocked as the rest of the city to learn that the new headquarters for LG Incorporated burned to the ground last night. From what I have heard through the media about the timing of the fire, I was in the building only a few hours earlier."

I cleared my throat again. "Leonard Goranson and I, along with our investment advisor Dina Rowland, went to the building after a cocktail party late Saturday night. Our purpose was to admire the plans one more time before the stock went on sale. A short while later, Ms. Rowland and I left together. Mr. Goranson may have left at any time after that. But I have not heard from him today, which is very unusual, and I expect the worst news when the debris is searched."

The next part was going to be hard, but it had been George's feeling that complete honesty was the best policy. I wanted to put this behind me, but everything I was about to say the tabloids could discover and keep in the headlines for weeks. I hadn't been able to consult Dina about it, but I felt certain, after the kiss she had given me in front of everyone at the cocktail party, that she would not object—that, in fact, she would applaud. I would have asked, but she'd been in a deep sleep from almost the moment we'd arrived at her apartment.

Her exhaustion was the exact opposite of my elation at finding myself free of the chains of despair.

"It will surprise many people to know that Leonard Goranson

and I were husband and wife." I let the buzz subside before I went on. "Our marriage was one of convenience and he required it of me before he would take me on as a model. I was not on the best terms with him. Ms. Rowland and I, as many people in her company found out last night, very recently began a romantic relationship." The buzz returned, much louder.

"I know that these facts would have come to light sooner or later and have no reason to withhold them. I am as dismayed by this turn of events as anyone, since Mr. Berkeley informs me, as did Ms. Rowland, that under the circumstances, the stock sale of LG Incorporated has been put on hold. If in fact Mr. Goranson died in the fire, it will be canceled. I am guessing that after debts are settled both here and in England, there will be very little left. The timing of this event could not have been worse for me, in the cold, hard light of day. My lack of grief will no doubt cause comment, but as I said before, I was not on good terms with Mr. Goranson. That is all I have to say to the press at this time. I am more than willing to cooperate with the investigating authorities should they require my assistance."

I stepped back, and the flashbulbs began again, accompanied by a crescendo of "Bella! Bella!"

"Why did you hate him? Did you want him dead? How much money did you lose?" The questions overlapped, and I answered none of them. George put his hand under my elbow and escorted me to the anteroom door.

"You were great," George said as soon as the door closed behind us. The Press Club staff would eventually clear the room.

I sat down, weak-kneed, and took a deep breath. "I'm not a good liar."

"You only lied about one thing—you know he's in there."

"And I know that he was unconscious when we left."

George's mouth tightened. "I didn't want to believe Dina. One of the few times my intuition let me down. I'm afraid her credibility is going to suffer. She should have known you were married to him and, considering your...relationship with her, that you would probably get a divorce, taking half his personal assets and half the business in England, which he owned."

I was shaking my head. "But I wouldn't have. I can produce the prenuptial agreement."

George grunted. "We'll have to see how it plays out in the financial press." He looked at his expertly shined shoes. "Are you really destitute?"

I grinned. "With friends like you, who could be destitute?"

He laughed, and again, to my surprise, I saw respect for me in his eyes. I hoped that I continued to have it.

George saw me into a cab from the club's discreet rear exit and told me to wish Dina a speedy recovery. As we made our way through midtown, I closed my eyes. I'd told George that Leo had turned violent when I'd informed him I was leaving him for Dina. He'd fallen during a struggle with Dina and hit his head. He was stunned, but very much alive when we ran, afraid for our own lives.

It was all based in truth, and yet of course it left out so many things. Unbelievable events. George Berkeley was not the kind of man to believe that Dina and I had been rescued by a spirit who had then lifted an incredible burden from my heart.

I really didn't believe it myself. Yet I couldn't deny I had been held by evil. Why was it so hard to believe that good had finally rescued me? Why is it easier to believe I had earned bad things, but not good ones? If it wasn't earned, it was easy to believe evil had chosen me randomly—then why couldn't good do the same?

Regardless, by design or chance, I was free. *Free.* I didn't know what to do with a future. But I knew where I wanted it to begin.

Reassured by the note that Christa had left, Dina decided a long, hot shower was definitely what the doctor ordered. In the bathroom she examined her burned hands and bruises. She looked like she'd walked away from a train wreck.

The burns were not as severe as they had seemed last night. Her skin was lightly pink, but there was no sign of the blisters. She had expected to feel like a used punching bag for a week, but she could contemplate physical activity. Certainly something pleasant when Christa returned.

Her mind told her not to take anything for granted. But her heart, after those incredible moments when she and Christa had shared the kiss for Rahdonee and Christabel, could not believe that Christa would not be back, and soon.

She dried her hair and rubbed moisturizer into every pore of her body. She had no idea what a future with Christa would be like. What would Christa do, now that she was free to do what she wanted? And what would work be like for Dina now that the investment that had earned her a partner's chair had gone up—literally—in smoke?

After a large mug of hot chocolate, she opened all the blinds and soaked in surprising and very welcome sunshine. She brought the glass with the sprouted roots to the table and stroked the bumps that promised more leaves. The touch still made her tingle, but that was all it was.

"You deserve a place in the sun," Dina told the plant. A place in the sun sounded just fine, but if she had the shortest partnership in Wall Street history, then a place in the sun, the kind of place she would want to share with Christa, well, it would be a long time coming. All at once she realized that where didn't matter. She and Christa would make their own sun wherever they went.

She sprang to answer the phone and tried to cover her disappointment when George, not Christa, was on the other end.

"I thought I'd get the machine," George said promptly. "Christa said that you were dead on your feet and that she couldn't bear to wake you."

"I was, just about. I'm glad she called you. But I haven't heard from her—what's going on?"

"It's a slow news day. Turn on CNN."

There was Christa, reading her statement as the latest breaking news on the "spectacular, early-morning" fire, courageously contained by firefighters," that had claimed the life of "one of the most fascinating new designers in the U.S." Christa was followed by shocked grief from the top employees in the U.K. operation. Then a fire department spokesman commented on how fortunate they were the fire had not spread far from its origin. They promised more information when any more was available.

"So, George, where does this leave you and me?" She supposed she should just face the music.

"Christa signed a prenup. Did you know that?"

"I'm not surprised. I didn't know they were married until a couple of days ago."

"So I suppose I can spin to our clients that you didn't have to reveal the possibility of a divorce because of the prenup, but..."

"I screwed up," she said into George's silence. "And people are going to be wary."

"You're going to have to face a partners' review. A week from now, I would guess, after the dust settles a bit."

"Okay." Her thoughts wandered to Christa. She had looked absolutely gorgeous on television.

"You don't sound worried."

"Of course I am. A week ago I would have been petrified. But I hate to tell you this, you're second banana from now on."

George let out an agonized groan. "Just rip my heart out, why don't you?"

"Sorry, that's the way it is."

George sighed. "And as it should be."

"George, you're a romantic! Who'd have thought?"

"Don't tell, and I'll make sure you keep your partner's chair. But you're going to have to work your hinder off to stay in it."

"Okay. Is that before or after I take a long vacation?"

"Put a sock in it, Dina. And don't come to work tomorrow— I'll handle the press that shows up. I'm sure they are already outside your door, so be prepared to make your statement and move on."

After George hung up, Dina saw that the answering machine's thirty-message memory was full. She listened to the first two reporters demanding information, then deleted the rest. She investigated why the doorbell hadn't been buzzing on over time and found that Christa had resourcefully turned it off. Smart girl, Dina thought. She called down to the doorman who confirmed that several reporters were hanging around. The phone rang, and a reporter left another message. A few minutes later another called.

Well, this wasn't going to be fun.

She stretched out on the sofa and closed her eyes. For a split second she saw Goranson's convulsed body as the flames from Christa's dress spread over him.

From far away, inside her mind, bells whispered, *He is the past. She is the future, all your futures.*

There was a knock at the door and Dina rose to peer through the security glass. A flash of red hair, a smile like moonrise—she pulled the door open.

The future spread out in front of her like an unpainted canvas. She became the canvas and a vibrant, laughing Christa dipped her hands into Green.

Epilogue

"Take a deep breath," Julia's photographer advised her.

"Shut up, Mickey," she snapped.

"Blow me, Julia."

She pushed open the building doors. After they gave their names to the receptionist, they had a few minutes to look around.

"Get some shots of the tree," Julia said.

Mickey was already setting up. "I know my freakin' job."

"I can do without the freakin' attitude." Photographers.

"Bite me." His camera whirred. Julia knew from experience Mickey wouldn't hear another word she said.

The tree was beautiful. She walked to the railing that circled it and looked down. When she'd read up for the interview, she'd learned that tons and tons of earth had been brought in to fill in at least one lower floor to give the gigantic oak sufficient room to grow. And grow it did. Ten years and it looked almost mature.

She had the weirdest urge to climb it.

She chided herself for the foolish impulse. This was the big time and in just a few minutes she would be interviewing two very influential women. Influential? Hell—rich, beautiful, famous and best of all, lesbian. No time for games.

She had lain awake most of the night mentally schooling herself to remain calm. This interview was her big break and was going to be a tremendous challenge.

The elevator doors opened behind her. She turned, hoping it would be an escort to the interview. Her composure was disrupted right away by the approach of Liza Brightly. God, the woman aged as beautifully as Katherine Hepburn. Julia felt like a gauche school girl by comparison. Liza still modeled, but her real contribution to the company was in management. Julia'd been warned that she managed people, particularly reporters, very well.

"It's a pleasure," Liza said. It sounded like an invitation to entirely inappropriate behavior. Wow.

Her handshake made Julia feel just a bit wobbly in the knees. Mickey took a picture of Liza in the elevator, and more as she led Julia through a maze of cubicles and hallways. As they approached the president's office, Julia was aware of how the light increased. The entire building was like that—light everywhere from skylights and picture windows. It was as if someone couldn't stand even a hint of shadow in spite of being right in the middle of one of the most densely populated places on the planet. And here, in front of the holy of holies, the office of Christabel herself, another skylight let in direct sunshine.

It made Julia want to go to the beach.

She pushed the irrelevant thought from her mind, only to moments later be completely discomfited by Liza Brightly's nearness as she turned back after knocking lightly on the door.

"When you're done I'd love to talk to you about your impressions," she breathed. "Maybe we could go for a drink?"

Wow. All Julia could think was *wow*. She nodded, praying Liza didn't notice she was goose pimples all over. Wow.

The door opened and a young woman peered out. There was a burst of music, which Julia recognized from a recent Christabel ad campaign. A man's voice pronounced, "It sucks! It just sucks!"

The young woman nodded to Liza, then gestured to Julia and

Mickey to follow her into the room.

There was a babble of voices, and then, as if a bell had rung, they fell silent. Julia paused in the doorway and let Christabel's contralto voice wash over her.

"No one is happy with the way this campaign is going, including me. The ship has sunk, so let's move on. Henry, you're absolutely right, it just sucks. Which means you bring the Thai food for tonight's creative session."

There was a burst of laughter and the rustle of people rising and collecting papers. Julia stopped just inside the door, taking in the magnificence of a huge mural. In the style of Chagall, it seemed to be a Native American scene, with teepees and a red-haired woman on a horse surrounded by vivid yellows, blues and greens.

Behind Julia a voice said, "Excuse me."

She stepped out of the way and—*wow*. Big wow. It was Dina Rowland. My God she couldn't believe she'd gotten this assignment. Dina Rowland walked like a goddess and Julia had to roll her tongue up off the carpet.

The young woman beckoned to her impatiently. She didn't seem phased at all. Julia supposed she was used to being around Dina and Christabel.

Mickey shoved past her and started taking pictures. He got a beaut right off, capturing Dina's first look at Christabel herself in the flesh.

The head of the multimillion dollar fashion machine sat on the end of a large desk, swinging her denim-clad legs and reading some papers.

Click and Mickey caught the transformation of her face as she looked up and saw Dina. From beautiful to rapturous. Jesus Christ. It had been ten years, and Christa looked at Dina as if she had just fallen in love.

Click and Mickey had a shot the tabloids would pay a fortune for. Julia would burn the negative herself. He swatted at Julia's hand as she covered his lens, preventing any photos of the next few moments.

Dina took Christa's face in her hands, and Christa wrapped her legs around Dina's thighs. The kiss was pure magic. Nope, Julia thought, I am never going to find anyone who loves me like that.

Then they were apart, and Mickey shoved Julia and went on taking pictures. The young woman was quite impatient now, so Julia stepped quickly toward the desk.

"Christa, this is Julia Rodriguez from *Fortune*. The ten-year anniversary article?"

Christabel nodded, and the young woman faded into the background, at least for Julia. Because then Christabel, in the flesh, smiled at her as she hopped down off the desk.

She was frozen in place. Dina held out her hand and Julia automatically shook it.

"Don't worry," Dina said, her tone friendly. "She does that to me, too."

Julia reminded herself that she was writing for a financial magazine. She had a long list of questions about the phenomenal success of Christabel/Phoenix, or CHRIX as it appeared on stock tickers. She was supposed to revisit how Christabel had decided to carry on with the initial designs created by her then-husband and surrounded herself with talented designers from around the world. How she had helped design this building over the ashes of the one that had burned down with her husband in it.

Julia's next questions were to deal with the business and personal partnership with the woman who had convinced a number of gun-shy investors to stick with the company even though the person at the helm had changed. As CHRIX expanded, Rowland's ability to manage capital and set up international partnerships had brought the haute couture Christabel line to Europe and had put upscale mass-market Phoenix designs in women's closets worldwide. Not only that, she had led the industry in setting workplace standards for suppliers in developing countries, and CHRIX was one of the first fashion-based corporations to Go Green. Just interviewing Dina could take days.

Mickey was snapping pictures. Christ, he was on his second

roll already. Julia sat down, recorder on, notebook poised, and steeled herself to look across the small conference table. It was overwhelming.

There's beauty that is mostly make-up and hair and nails and clothes that say, "Look at me, I'm beautiful."

And there's the kind of beauty that just is. Julia thought suddenly of the timeless oak tree in the atrium, and she thought of the last time, way too long ago, that she'd stood all by herself in the open air, and heard the wind moving through the trees.

Christabel said, "I believe you have some questions for us."

Their fingers were intertwined on the table, as if they were never really parted.

Julia was supposed to ask about the next ten years and their business projections in the field of women's attire.

Instead she asked, "What's it like to be so in love?"

Publications from
Bella Books, Inc.
The best in contemporary lesbian fiction

P.O. Box 10543, Tallahassee, FL 32302
Phone: 800-729-4992
www.bellabooks.com

WITHOUT WARNING: Book one in the Shaken series by KG MacGregor. Without Warning is the story of their courageous journey through adversity, and their promise of steadfast love.
ISBN: 978-1-59493-120-8 $13.95

THE CANDIDATE by Tracey Richardson. Presidential Candidate Jane Kincaid had always expected the road to the White House would exact a high personal toll. She just never knew how high until forced to choose between her heart and her political destiny.
ISBN: 978-1-59493-133-8 $13.95

TALL IN THE SADDLE by Karin Kallmaker, Barbara Johnson, Therese Szymanski and Julia Watts. The playful quartet that penned the acclaimed Once Upon A Dyke and Stake Through the Heart are back are now turning to the Wild (and Very Hot) West to bring you another collection of erotically charged, action-packed, tales.
ISBN: 978-1-59493-106-2 $15.95

IN THE NAME OF THE FATHER by Gerri Hill. In this highly anticipated sequel to Hunter's Way, Dallas Homicide Detectives Tori Hunter and Samantha Kennedy investigate the murder of a Catholic priest who is found naked and strangled to death.
ISBN: 978-1-59493-108-6 $13.95

IT'S ALL SMOKE AND MIRRORS: The First Chronicles of Shawn Donnelly by Therese Szymanski. Join Therese Szymanski as she takes a walk on the sillier side of the gritty crime scene detective novel and introduces readers to her newest alternate personality—Shawn Donnelly.
ISBN: 978-1-59493-117-8 $13.95

THE ROAD HOME by Frankie J. Jones. As Lynn finds herself in one adventure after another, she discovers that true wealth may have very little to do with money after all.
ISBN: 978-1-59493-110-9 $13.95

IN DEEP WATERS: CRUISING THE SEAS by Karin Kallmaker and Radclyffe. Book passage on a deliciously sensual Mediterranean cruise with tour guides Radclyffe and Karin Kallmaker.
ISBN: 978-1-59493-111-6 $15.95

ALL THAT GLITTERS by Peggy J. Herring. Life is good for retired Army Colonel Marcel Robicheaux. Marcel is unprepared for the turn her life will take. She soon finds herself in the pursuit of a lifetime—searching for her missing mother and lover.
ISBN: 978-1-59493-107-9 $13.95

OUT OF LOVE by KG MacGregor. For Carmen Delallo and Judith O'Shea, falling in love proves to be the easy part.
ISBN: 978-1-59493-105-5 $13.95

BORDERLINE by Terri Breneman. Assistant Prosecuting attorney Toni Barston returns in the sequel to Anticipation.
ISBN: 978-1-59493-99-7 $13.95

PAST REMEMBERING by Lyn Denison. What would it take to melt Peri's cool exterior? Any involvement on Asha's part would be simply asking for trouble and heartache...wouldn't it?
ISBN: 978-1-59493-103-1 $13.95

ASPEN'S EMBERS by Diane Tremain Braund. Will Aspen choose the woman she loves...or the forest she hopes to preserve...
ISBN: 978-1-59493-102-4 $14.95

THE COTTAGE by Gerri Hill. The Cottage is the heartbreaking story of two women who meet by chance . . . or did they? A love so destined it couldn't be denied . . . stolen moments to be cherished forever.
ISBN: 978-1-59493-096-6 $13.95

FANTASY: Untrue Stories of Lesbian Passion edited by Barbara Johnson and Therese Szymanski. Lie back and let Bella's bad girls take you on an erotic journey through the greatest bedtime stories never told.
ISBN: 978-1-59493-101-7 $15.95

SISTERS' FLIGHT by Jeanne G'Fellers. SISTERS FLIGHT is the highly anticipated sequel to NO SISTER OF MINE and SISTER LOST SISTER FOUND
ISBN: 978-1-59493-116-1 $13.95

BRAGGIN RIGHTS by Kenna White. Taylor Fleming is a thirty-six year old Texas rancher who covets her independence. She finds her cowgirl independence tested by neighboring rancher Jen Holland.
ISBN: 978-1-59493-095-9 $13.95